GRADUATION INTO THE COSMOS

GRADUATION INTO THE COSMOS

A NOVEL

LOU BALDIN

GRADUATION INTO THE COSMOS

ISBN: 978-1-329-91113-0

Table of Contents

PROLOG 12

MY LAST DAY ON EARTH 15

COLOSSAL STAR CLUSTER............................26

MASSIVE CREATURES ROAMED THE PLANET........51

STRANGE AND WONDERFUL PLANET 78

SINGING CITIES..111

ORIGIN OF SOULS 116

COSMIC RHYME 140

LIFE AS A SPIRIT..142

SPACE-AGE EARTH...156

UTOPIA AND SEXUALITY 164

FLEET OF CARRIAGES......................................184

BOOKS BY THE AUTHOR...................................199

BLOGS IN BOOK FORM 200

PROLOG

What be these fragile bodies we live inside? Transports of forgotten and lost souls eternally enslaved by restless spirits, dammed and tormented in an endless search for peace, happiness, and joy. Each soul in a constant and hectic pursuit to reconnect with something grand lost a long time ago. We mortals, in our mindless travels through life, grasping at, reaching for and attempting, often in vain, to understand what purpose we are created, and by whom. Senseless it seems the torturous journey to understand the imposing plan if there even be such a plan.

Reincarnation is an idea that has been debated by civilized people before the beginning of recorded history. Today, people's views on the subject are as varied as their religious beliefs and their hidden desires. In modern times, many people have come forward with their experiences of the phenomena called reincarnation. Claiming that they remember living a life in other centuries, and other places, and as other people. The author of this book is one such person, with memories of past lives; and attempts to express and describe bits and pieces of the reality that exist in the collective minds of souls, existing in this vast and never-ending universe. Such tidbits can only scratch the surface of the things mortals can expect to experience when they leave this planet permanently.

I tell this story from the perspective of a character, a man (not the author), who made the transition from life on Earth, and moved into the realms "above" the gods. A path walked by all souls, great and small that manage to rip away from the bonds of the physical realm that have a strong luring and ensnaring quality, that dauntingly draws on the souls of mankind and beckoning them to stay. It takes a strong persevering desire to break free from the chains of materialistic delusions that all souls on this plane of existence have succumbed.

We go through life hiding our shame, insecurities, ignorance and hate while in the cover of the flesh. Covering our flaws with comfortable garments to keep us warm, secure, and respectable around our peers, while hiding a dubious and fractured soul. After we die, we are naked in the universe, free from our body and no longer able to hide even the smallest of blemishes, glaring back at us from our exposed souls.

We die with our clothes on and awaken in the afterworld, naked.

MY LAST DAY ON EARTH

"Holy crap! I'm a dead man!" My last words out of my mouth when I saw a car careening out of control and me and my car were directly in its path. Then mind-numbing darkness.

I died today and received my life review soon after. I was told it was my last and "final" day on Earth (as a human), having broken the chains from a long and torturous reincarnation cycle. I was now free to move higher into the cosmic realms and explore the wonders of the universe for the rest of my perpetual existence.

During my final review, I was shown a portion of my past and the tormented lives that I had lived and died from on Earth, and on other planets too.

I was astounded by the depth of details placed before me, and presented to me, concerning many of my previous lives. Lives in which I believed long gone and had hoped would go away forever. I didn't know about them up until that moment of near-total recall and then realized I had many such death-interviews about my past lives. Which always left me mystified (the interviews), yet hopeful that lives would permanently erase and not torment me in future lives. But none of my previous interviews were as detailed as this final debriefing, and the realization that came with it of the permanency of past lives.

To my dismay, it was all there in front of me, and to my horror, undisputable. Until my death, and my subsequent life review, I had no idea that I had been alive in other lives; besides the one I had just died from. It was remarkable that nothing from my past lives leaked into my mind and presented me with evidence or hints that life was so pervasive, and filled with so many complex interactions with other people in other realities.

Memories of each lifetime and every gory detail connected with each lifetime flooded my boggled mind the moment my death-guide opened the secret compartment where resided a reservoir of information; neatly stuffed inside one of my many hidden cubbyholes inside of my soul. From where, apparently, most everything about me was stored for all time (or thereabouts) to be rummaged through during life reviews. Or whenever superior souls felt the need to rub your nose into some errant details in your life.

The capacity of my mind/soul was enormous and reminded me of the mountainous landfill in the large city that I lived in before I died. I could never escape the smell or the ugly sight of that ever-growing eyesore, which was plainly visible from the freeway when driving to work each morning. (I was able to see so many things all at once inside of my personal landfill regrettably forever entrenched inside of my soul.) Whether I wanted to see it or not (and I didn't want to). There was no escaping it, no flooring the gas pedal to get away from it, as I sometimes did when driving my car past the landfill to ditch the smell.

To my surprise, nothing was lost in the transition from one life to the next life, and yet, I remained clueless about the people and the lives that I recently left behind. (Now that I was no longer part of their lives.) But that would change as I acclimated to my new reality in the land of the dead.

Free of my confining human body, my mind was able to see and know so many things about myself and the things about the world that I spent so much time on; and mostly in a confused state of mind. The information was always there, tucked away in my soul, in hibernation to one day be used against me or in my defense, on my day of reckoning, as I recently reckoned with.

The journey I was about to embark on wouldn't become clear to me immediately, or shortly after my death either. My guide advised me that there was so much he would reveal to me over a period and through my adventures away from my physical body (and the physical world I had become accustomed to). The information would slowly unfold and embrace me over the course of my growing awareness of the things around me and in my emerging reality.

I learned from my guide that this universe was only one of many that I would evolve in and through, and eventually out of, at some point during my existence. For now, in my emerging new reality, I would enjoy exploring this portion of reality for my preparation for a larger and extended veracity of truth to follow. One that I would also move out of when I was ready to be released from each stage, and further explore the ever reaching and higher pastures of awareness.

At some point after my life review, I was shown things that transpired after my death at the crash site. My body, removed from the mangled wreckage that used to be my car, was placed onto a stretcher by paramedics at the scene. My body was then placed into a waiting ambulance and taken to the city morgue.

I died in the accident. My body was a bloody mess, and the paramedics were unable to stop the bleeding or revive my corpse due to the severity of my injuries.

I was alone in the car that morning and driving to an early morning meeting at my office. On my way to the office, I had no inkling, no gut feeling that something was about to unfold and forever change my focus and the direction of my existence. In an instant, a car that was traveling in the opposite direction that my car was traveling, and going at a high rate of speed, ran off the road and then jerked back onto the road, hitting my car head-on. The crash demolished both vehicles in an explosion of metal and chunks of pavement that were knocked loose by the horrendous impact of the two cars.

Miraculously, the driver of the car that hit me walked away physically unscratched. Mentally, he was devastated, and forever damaged after seeing the accident that he had caused to happen by his carelessness.

The driver swerved to miss a pothole in the road and over-corrected and hit my car. Had he not been speeding he could have avoided the accident. The driver will carry the burdened of my death for the rest of his life (I heard from my guide). I was not a vengeful person and wished him no harm or revenge for causing my death. If it were in my power I would have relieved him of his guilt-ridden affliction, but I could not.

I died instantly from the collision and felt no pain because my soul was removed from my convulsing body moments after the impact, by a death guide (Grim Reaper). After my death, and Grim's work done, Grim left and another guide replaced him. The new guide's job was to escort me to a place nearby a massive star system that was close to the center of the Milky Way galaxy. I didn't know either of the guides or whatever they were, nor could I see them clearly but I could hear them talking to me, and to each other, in my mind, telepathically. They both seemed to know every detail about me and my life. The guides performed their duties nonchalantly and as routinely and efficiently as if they were mere machines on an assembly line.

FRIGHTENING PLACE

In a flash of light, the guide and I traveled to a place away from Earth and arrived in an instant to a monumental structure somewhere out in the darkness of space. The guide and I entered a cavernous area inside of the building or spaceship or whatever it was. What it was, was cold, or looked to be. I didn't feel cold, but the place was dark and dreary like the inside of a damp cave, and it gave me shivers, even though I didn't have a body. I don't see much of anything, but I heard moans and screams echoing somewhere deep inside the cavern.

Deeper inside of the cavern I didn't see anyone or anything only heard the same strange human and animal sounds getting closer. My guide remained quiet about the eerie noises, and I didn't ask him about the distant commotion, even though I wanted too. I follow him through one of the several corridors inside of the massive cavern, filled with tubes and tunnels that looked like large and twisted spaghetti-like structures. The corridor twisted and turned inside one of the tubes and emptied into a larger space that housed big, round, glass tubes. The upright tubes appeared filled with a colorful and glowing liquid that lit up the otherwise darkness in that place. The strange liquid was churning and agitating like the inside of a washing machine.

Odd looking beings (creatures) were inside of each of the glass containers. I saw one creature per tube. The beings looked humanoid with two legs, two arms, a midsection and head, but they were not human. The full-grown beings inside the tubes were suspended in the fluid and looked as if they were asleep (their eyes closed).

The room was enormous and crammed full of the strange glass tubes. The creatures inside of the tubes were taller than the average human, perhaps nine or ten feet tall. My guide and I continued passed the tubes/containers and went towards where the screams emanated.

I broke my silence and asked my guide "where are we and why am I being shown this place?" He fails to answer me, and we continued as if on a tour of a house of horrors.

We reached an area where human-looking people were standing around and looking all confused and fearful. I didn't see any animals, which I was expecting because I believed that's what I heard when we first entered this place. The guide was no help and didn't clarify for me what the animal sounds were. But he did say it had nothing to do with me and where I was going. That was a relief!

The humans were milling about in an enclosed glassed-in part of the building that was well lit. The glass partitioned enclosure didn't appear to have doors or other openings other than it had no ceiling and was open at the top. The glass walls were about ten feet high and the people inside them all less than six feet tall, about the size of average humans. I estimated that there were about a hundred people inside that one glass cage that we first saw. There were many other similar enclosed holding pens in that area, some that were empty and others with various quantities of people inside of them. The cubed glass containers seemed randomly dispersed throughout that large space.

Some of the people were walking around in the enclosures; others were sitting on the floor or just standing like statues. Many of them were staring off as if in a state of shock and confusion. A few were wailing, crying, and screaming that they "don't want to go." My guide speaks and tells me that these people are about to be placed into new bodies, bodies made with the DNA from their former carcasses, which had died. Unlike me, they were still in possession of their dead bodies. They were dead and awaiting new bodies. Their souls hadn't ascended (departed) from their old bodies at the moment of death. The souls were unhappy about that and their pending destination.

I was horrified at the sight! With a sense of foreboding, I asked my guide why some of these people were distressed while others were not, or didn't act like they were or didn't care about their freakish circumstances. "Were they being sent to different realities, planets, places, to Hades or worse?" He said they were. I was hesitant to ask more questions that I didn't particularly want to know the answers. Not while I was in that place and fearful that my guide was going to lock me up in one of those glass holding pens.

"Life in this galaxy is far from being chaotic and random, as is believed my so many people on Earth. All lives have a purpose, design, and an outcome. The outcome, the consequences, for those people in the glass enclosures were scheduled to begin." Said my guide. Who also said that, "every moment in human lives, every choice determines a new destiny in this universe."

I asked, "Don't people die first? These people looked like they are alive, yet they are in their street clothes and are in their physical human dead bodies." His response, "They have died and have been kept inside their corpses until placed into their new appropriate bodies. Bodies suited for their next destination, next life."

While at that unpleasant place, I received a physical body too and was told it was a temporary body.

How temporary was contingent on my ability to progress through the labyrinth of stages I would process through in other places and on other planets.

Up to that moment, I was in spirit form without a physical body. My earth body, I had left on Earth, to rot, to decompose. I was then handed off to yet another being/guide who was a bit more mysterious and much more elusive than the last one. He took me to another place in the Milky Way galaxy. I remained unsure of where I was going and was not optimistic, having seen some of my less than perfect, past lives.

COLOSSAL STAR CLUSTER

There were thousands of massive stars in the cluster. The trip seemed instantaneous, yet I could see it unfold in front of me and was fully aware of the approach; even while I traveled at a high rate of speed towards my destination. As we neared the breath-taking glow of thousands of bright stars, which made up the star cluster, my bewildered soul was in a state of exhilaration. The brightness of the stars was far beyond stupendous, and the sight left my mind dazed. I was stunned by the magnitude of luminosity engulfing the space around the stars! The illumination was so intense and so bright that it left little room for darkness to hide in the vastness of space that was between the stars inside of the star cluster.

The star system was somewhere in the center of the star cluster. And we passed through the innards of the star cluster that went on forever or would have if we were only traveling at the speed of light. We traveled many multiples of light speed, and I beheld a place that was remarkably large and mind-numbingly intense. As we pushed through many colorful waves and layers of energy, and I realized, I was not headed to Hades, and what a relief that was! The journey itself through the wonderland of thousands of stars lit up my soul like a firefly. It was as if

I had entered a dense forest of stars, surreal, so dreamlike, and so intoxicating!

The space around us glowed brightly as did my supernatural guide. In my excitement, I'm sure I did a bit of glowing too. My guide was mostly invisible, but whenever he phased into view, into my reality, which wasn't often, he was as blindingly bright as the stars that we flew past.

I could not see what my guide looked like only felt immense and generous joy emanating from him, it or her. I was unable to know or distinguish the guide's gender or race or even if it had such limiting human qualities and attributes as gender and race. It didn't matter to me who or what it was, only that I liked this place a lot!

We paused briefly at a star system (my destination), and I soon found myself hovering over one of the planets belonging to that star. Then we were on the planet and inside one of the large buildings on that planet. The guide did something to my body, made some adjustment to it, and my body felt a bit heavier and more alive than during my travel to this place. It wasn't a body change only a denser and better-suited adjustment for the new place/planet I was going to be on. "The previous version of your body was more suited for rapid travel through space," said my guide. I didn't feel like I was traveling inside of an orb or some ship nor the mode of my travel.

Mentally, I felt the same as I did as a human on Earth before I died. Except now I had no body aches or needs of any kind troubling or pestering me or my temporary body. From what I could tell, and I wasn't able to tell much about anything, the body I was inside of looked similar to my old body that I left on Earth to rot. I could not see my body clear enough to know, so I wasn't sure. I could feel my arms, legs, torso and head as if it were my old body, the one I carried around on Earth until it died.

Movement in this new location and reality was peculiar and fascinating. Things and places simply happened without my knowing what triggered them to happen. I had no idea what I wanted or where to go without input from my attendant (guide). But I wasn't sure I still had a guide because there was so little direction/communication, supplied to me. Nevertheless, I supposed that I was still under the control of a mysterious escort of some kind. One that managed to remain out of sight during most of our voyage to this place, and after we arrived; except for momentarily appearing to adjust my bodysuit and then quickly disappeared afterward.

My escort was like a parent pulling up a toddlers pants whenever they slipped down. Perhaps the guide remained out of view to give me a feeling of freedom, some elbow room and let me think I had a bit of control of my new situation. He did drop the occasional hint that she was there hiding in the background somewhere, into my otherwise confused and slightly disoriented mind.

My mind remained far clearer than any time when I was on Earth, but this place was something far different than three-dimensional Earth, and more like swimming through multiple dimensions of time and space. That created substantial confusion that took some adjusting.

At least I knew without a doubt that a guide, chaperon, attendant, babysitter or whatever they are, existed. Unlike when I was on Earth, where I had no clue or idea about spirit beings (guides or whatnot) nor did I believe in the afterlife. All that rapidly changed after my car accident. And now I'm awakened to the most fantastic, bizarre and yet, somewhat terrifying existence. An existence that was swiftly unfolding before me in every direction, and as gentle and as orderly as a tornado.

I had family back on Earth, elderly parents and a few uncles and aunts; no children, spouse or girlfriends. I was oblivious to the people I had left behind (unaware of them) ever since I arrived at this peculiar place in the cosmos. I was concerned about how my parents might have handled my sudden and unexpected death. I had no sense of time or even it time existed where I was now, which gave me no bearing on how long ago I had passed away. I wanted to say goodbye or communicate something to them but wasn't given the chance, yet.

I had a few friends on Earth, none that was close or dear to me. Mostly associates that I worked with and occasionally had a beer with after work at a local pub.

I was interested in a girl that worked in the office with me, and I was planning to ask her out, had I not died. Lucky for her, since apparently my time was due to run out. The rulers of the universe spared her from knowing me on a personal and intimate level and saving her from having her heart broken by my sudden death (had a relationship developed between us). She did act interested in me, and I showed some interest in her, but neither of us made much effort to connect.

I didn't believe in destiny while I was alive back on Earth. I now know that life on Earth has a definite meaning and an extremely puzzling design to it.

The guide mentioned to me that everyone must endeavor to find a purpose in life so that they can fulfill a hidden and personal desire/destiny, and meet certain criteria before they can leave the confines of three-dimensional existence; and the corresponding 'marry-go-round" existence of reincarnation. Which apparently, I had managed to do this time around.

Anger and envy pestered me throughout many of my past lives, and I succeeded in overpowering those two problems during my last two lives on Earth, according to my companion (who chimed in every once in a while).

I died young, in my early thirties, and had a good enough and mostly carefree life. During my life review session, I was told that I had met my cosmic goals and that I had achieved the bulk of my necessary escape credentials, during a previous life.

In that previous to my last life, I was a soldier in a war situation and was killed while saving the lives of a civilian family, caught in the crossfires during a gun battle to liberate a French village (in the First World War). I was twenty-two years old when I died in that life, a very short lifetime, one of my shortest lifetimes in my collection of past lives, I was told by my guide. I was destined to come back to Earth two or three decades after that life, to fix a few minor infractions that I incurred as a teenager before being drafted into that war. I have no recall of what I did while in that in-between-lives zone, before coming back to Earth for my last tour of duty as a human.

Now I feasted on two realities at the same time, memories from my previous lives, and the peeling away of layers of my new adventure, as a free soul, which began unfolding soon after my arrival in the afterlife. It was an absolute delight reliving precious past moments on Earth (I did manage to make a few), all the while anticipating and exploring the foretold (by my escort) nuggets of pleasure that lay before me like a galactic Easter egg hunt.

Soon after my arrival on planet Paradise, numerous partially invisible beings that showed up as vibrant wisps of energy that spun around me like swirls of colored sugar inside of a cotton candy machine greeted me. I was unaware of how many of them there were or what motivated them. My chaperon said nothing about them other than the mysterious wisps were glad to see me.

As moments passed the numbers of such wispy beings seemed to increase and sometimes became flurries of whirling indiscernible energy. I couldn't see them as much as I could feel their presence around me. Each wisp of energy (being) broadcasted unique frequencies of bliss and kindness towards me (gifts at a baby shower?). I was new and innocent to this place; childlike and naïve about the sheer and overwhelming strangeness that enveloped me. I felt coddled like a newborn baby.

The highly odd and rapidly moving beings came and went at supersonic speeds, greeting me without communicating verbally or telepathically, at least not on a level I was able to comprehend at that time. They didn't stick around long and left as quickly as they arrived. I pondered on who they could be; angels, relatives, friends or long lost and forgotten cosmic spirits that were crashing the party? And welcoming me to this new reality. I didn't know if I knew them, but I cherished the moments they spent with me, whoever the well-wishers were.

I no longer had a corruptible physical body as I had back on Earth, but I did have a physical body. The body they placed me into was indestructible and with the same features, shape, and size as the one that I had back on Earth. I walked, talked (to myself) and looked (?) like the man I used to be before I died. I assumed but had no mirror to verify what I looked like in the exterior. It was a physical body but not made of skin and bones as my old body was. My body was of a substance unlike anything imaginable on Earth, other than the body of the fictional Superman.

The body was flawless, magical and had incredible vitality. I could do everything I did on Earth and a whole lot more, without working up perspiration and becoming exhausted. Whatever I pleased to do I was told I could go out and do it. That realization seemed incredible and very liberating. To know that the universe is my oyster and has no equal when it comes to realizing the enormity of the privileges every soul in this existence is endowed. Which so far, I only had tasted a few crumbs of the feast that was beckoning me.

I began my departure from the building where my escort worked, and I headed down many diverting and intersecting hallways. On my way out of the maze, I ran into my guide, who advised me that he wasn't coming with me, said he had others like me that he was going to interact with, and promptly left the building ahead of me. I followed him out the door and watched him disappear into the crowd of people filling the sidewalks. And I dove into the crowds myself. I still never got a good look at my guide, he, she or it, seemed to want to remain incognito as much as possible. I was kind of happy to be free of the escort, though I appreciated immensely the guidance, the little I received.

The city reminded me of where I came from before death took me to this parallel universe. I walked around to get a feel of what the afterlife had to offer and discovered it was a lot like the city, the world I left behind. The hustle and bustle were very familiar to me.

Air existed on the planet, but I didn't need to breathe the air to live, or breathe air at all. I didn't require food or drink, but I could indulge if I wished in the exotic foods and beverages available for the taking, throughout the city. I seemed to know a lot of the details of that place.

The city was beyond fabulous, enticing and welcoming. It was stunningly gorgeous and clean, and made me feel as if I belonged there, which was unlike what I felt back on Earth, in the city I lived in; I never felt like I belong on Earth.

On Earth, I lived a modest lifestyle, drove a used car, and my pad (apartment) was less than spectacular. I had the money to live a better and richer life but never saw the need or had any desire to do so. The world for me was drab and boring. I knew that was mostly my fault, but there was so little that interested me on Earth. Earth had many exciting places, but they were so far from where I lived, and I hated traveling.

Deep down inside of me I knew I was not a creature of Earth. I felt alien to that planet and yet I didn't believe there was anything more to this universe when I was alive. I enjoyed looking up at the stars every once in a while when I was out and away from the haze of city lights, which wasn't often. I was a loner, always searching for something but never knew what that something was. I have finally found that something. The afterlife!

What a contrast from Earth this place was. On this planet, the city streets were made of Safire, and the sidewalks made of diamonds. The lampposts were mesmerizing and coated with precious stones and jewels, which gave sparkle and color that put a pep in my steps. On Earth, the streets were made of asphalt and were pothole havens, and depressing places to be during rush hour traffic jams.

The buildings on this planet were a rainbow-tinted translucent material, and many of the buildings reached into the sky far above the ground level and above the few clouds that occasionally drifted through the skies. Cloud cover was rare, and the skies were nearly always sunny.

Footprints of the larger buildings covered several city blocks and were so enormously huge that I felt like an insect in a forest of Sequoia trees when looking up.

Transportation was similar to Earth and consisted of elevated trains and subways, buses, horse-drawn carriages, cabs and pod-like cars that drove themselves. Everything was self-operating, driverless and mechanized. Planes, helicopters and hovering craft of various and peculiar designs filled the skies. Vehicles of every sort ferried people to mysterious places that only the passenger(s) would be privy to know. Somehow I knew that.

The only noise I heard in the city was soothing, enjoyable music, the kind that I liked. The music was everywhere as if piped in just for me. I didn't hear or notice the chatter of people talking or the screaming sirens of police, fire and ambulance vehicles. I didn't see such types of vehicles and certainly didn't miss the noise. That was mostly the kind of city clamor that kept me up late at night back on Earth. Attempting to get some sleep in my busy and noise-laden city was often futile.

The music that pervaded the area was music that I enjoyed when I was a human. Presumably, everyone heard only the music "they" enjoyed and wanted to hear. One of my pet peeves on Earth was neighbors in my building playing loud and obnoxious music, the kind of racket I didn't like. This place was like heaven in comparison.

I saw people doing what people do in the hustle and bustle of large cities back on Earth. Going to and fro with briefcases, shopping bags, and books and going about their business and doing familiar activities as back on Earth.

It didn't make sense to me. Why were people carrying that kind of mundane stuff around on this utopia planet? I saw smartphones, computer bags, and backpacks too. People were sitting on park benches reading newspapers or gazing into IPads or some other strange looking devices that I had never seen before and had no idea what they were. The whole thing didn't add up. Hot-dog stands and food carts and other strange looking contraptions where people stopped and got something to eat and drink, were on every corner, and most of them were very busy, and doing a great business. Except for the fact, I never noticed any money exchanging hands or the swiping of credit cards. That was different. I certainly didn't have any money, credit cards, loose change or even a wallet. And I didn't feel like I needed any such things in paradise.

I quickly picked up on the fact that people were doing the things that made them feel comfortable. Some recently and newly arrived souls were holding on to things that made them feel normal back on Earth, and normal here too. Like security blankets, they held tightly to old habits and devices that they loved and cherished and couldn't live without, back on Earth, and apparently here as well.

I saw joggers, running and bikers riding bikes along the pathways around a large body of water, a lake that was across the street from the large building where I was standing and waiting for the tram. The people all had incorruptible bodies as I did that needed no exercise, food or drink. All the things they loved doing or felt the need to do back on Earth, was happening here in the land of ecstasy. I didn't see anyone playing harps. That would have made more sense to me.

Apparently breaking free from earth doesn't equate to breaking free from the habits picked up on Earth. I learned that there was a transition period, and most of the cities were places where new souls transitioned from their lingering habits and hang-ups until they felt comfortable about leaving them behind. Once free, they could get serious and begin their progress to other places in the cosmic order.

Some people were old looking in their new bodies. Because they had not made the mental adjustment to the fact that age had no hold or bearing on their soul, especially now and in this place. Souls are ageless and eternal after they make their escape from lowlife planets.

I boarded a tram that required no fare and sat by a woman who looked about my age, and I wondered if I should strike up a conversation with her.

She looked at me, and I looked at her, both of us looking unsure of ourselves. Not a word exchanged between us. I decided to remain quiet. I was fine with that, and she seemed to be too. The tram was half-full of people, who were similar to us, at least looked like us, all quiet, almost as if everyone was in a meditation stupor. Which was understandable being that all of us were probably new or fairly new arrivals from Earth, or from some other planet?

From the window on the tram, I could see larger sections of the city. The city looked fairly normal with shops, offices, condos and apartment buildings covering much of the landscape.

After circling the city in the tram a few times, I exited the tram at one of the stops near where I had originally boarded. Walked around the town and noticed for the first time that some of the people were flying in the skies above me. Not with wings or a cape like Superman, just humans flying, floating, hovering surfing or whatever, through the air. Not surprisingly, knowing that things like that are or should be common happenings in the strangeness of the afterlife.

I was agnostic back in the human world and didn't believe in any religion or anything else with a paranormal slant. But now that I know life goes on after death I was kind of expecting to see angels flying around or sitting near a harp and playing a heavenly tune. But I didn't see any angels, seraphs or cherubs unless some of the people flying above were such things in human disguise.

The flying people looked like plain humans to me. My eyesight was keen, and I was able to see "somethings" even at distances, very well. A huge improvement from when I was on Earth, and wore glasses, which I did my whole life while on Earth. Couldn't see without my glasses. I didn't have or need glasses now. That was a huge relief and one of the countless benefits of being in this place, perfect vision. The fast moving beings that started swirling around me soon after I arrived and continued to do so remained a blur but nearly everything else I could see with little problem. So I thought.

I walked around the town the whole day, or the whole week, or the whole month. I had no idea of time or how long or how far I walked. I wasn't tired, hungry or thirsty. I did pass several restaurants, and food carts during my marathon walk, but never once felt the urge or need for food and drink.

I wasn't a spirit. I had a physical body, and the city had many tantalizing food places that were all waffling their mouthwatering aroma that lingered near each food establishment; beckoning me, daring me, to partake. There was no doubt in my mind that this was a Shangri-La of a planet, despite the discrepancies I mentioned earlier.

Having restaurants in this place made absolutely no sense to me unless they were for the permanent residents, the people that worked in the city and kept things moving and functioning for us recently dead people. However, I saw no evidence of people working anywhere. Robotics seemed to have all the labor requirements of the city, covered. The physical bodies of the arrivals to this place operated on some mysterious energy that existed in a body that needed no recharging.

Questions in my mind tended to answer themselves, eventually. But I was in no hurry for all the answers to come. I was having too much fun and wasn't sure I wanted any answers that would shorten or dampen the fun or the mystery.

My walk through parts of the marvelous city jarred my senses into overdrive. The ecstasy of sights and sounds of the vibrant city pulverized any lingering sadness ignited by my thoughts on leaving loved ones behind on Earth. I almost felt guilty for my lack of sadness, but hard as I tried to be sad, it was near impossible to overcome my giddy delight of being on that planet.

Cities large and small made up the landscape of that massive planet. A planet that was roughly the size of Jupiter, if not much larger. It was a solid planet, not a gas giant planet as Jupiter is supposed to be.

Knowledge crept in or seeped into my mind like ocean waves washing up new sand onto a beach. I was accumulating information as I needed it from my environment, virtually nonstop.

Crystalized cities surrounded by vast stretches of rainforest with trees larger that the Sequoia, in California. Lakes and waterways nestled in the enchanted forests where lived tamed and wild animals of every conceivable kind imaginable, and unimaginable, roamed free.

Rivers flowed through the land, fed from snowcapped towering mountains that reached into the sky as beacons of imposing grandeur. Rivers from the melting snow that capped the mountains meandered through the forests and the cities on their way towards the seas and the oceans, which covered large portions of the land, as such large bodies of water do on Earth.

People lived on waterfront properties, some in mansions like the rich and famous on Earth. No one here was famous that I could tell, but everyone was certainly rich in material goods, whether they wanted to be or not. Boats, yachts, and ships floated on all the places where water was. Large massive cruise ships plied the seas and the oceans, stopping at ports and vacation spots all around the planet. Ostentatious was alive and well in this corner of the Milky Way galaxy. And no one was complaining, just walking around in total amazement and awe of it all.

Back on Earth, I often felt embarrassed when I purchased something expensive and luxurious. Which I rarely did because of my feelings of guilt that overwhelmed me for my perceived flagrant extravagances. I could never in my wildest dreams fathom a place, a universe that was so fabulously wealthy in all things desirable, with no shortages of any kind. People of Earth have been seriously hoodwinked about the evils of extravagant living. Poverty, despair, war, hate and envy were the only things missing on this paradise of a planet.

Everything was free. Machines did all the work, and people did all the fun. The planet was the very definition of a utopia planet. No sickness, no aging, no children but everyone here was child-like in their enthusiasm for adventure and their penchant for finding fun in everything they did. People here soon found out that fun was in everything they chose to do. It took longer for some people to open up and take notice that they were no longer on Earth, and could begin enjoying themselves without the guilt they had learned to embrace back on Earth.

Storms, hurricanes, tornadoes, earthquakes, floods and typhoons were nonexistent on this planet. There were elements of weather, but they didn't dampen or interrupt anything people did or wanted to do. The rain knew when and where to fall. As did the snow.

Food as that found on Earth was farmed and harvested by machines on vast farms both above ground and in underground caverns. Caverns so large that massive cities could easily have stacked inside of them, and did. Cities bejeweled the Swiss cheese like caverns throughout the interior of the enormously large planet, like crystals inside of rocks.

My only fear was that I would wake up and find that all of it was a dream. Luckily I never woke up; I only continued to move higher into the cosmic wonderland with every activity. On Earth, most people lived their whole lives scarcely awake and always dreading, and fearing their lives and the uncertain future. With good reason, for Earth is a fearful place for a lot of people. Where misfortune, disease, dread, wars and blatant lies, perpetuated and kept alive by the rulers and the clergy of the land, existed. The kind of pretenses that helped keep many people in a state of hate, confusion, envy and guilt.

Some people had the ability to fly, and others didn't. I walked, took the bus, trains, planes, boats, and biked on the trails. Until I realized that I too could fly, and then that was all I did. Mostly.

Back on earth, my favorite dreams were those where I flew like a bird and swooped down through unfamiliar places and enjoyed the magnificent views from the air. I loved those dreams! Humans couldn't fly on Earth without mechanical constructs of some kind. On this planet, humans were flying like birds without any mechanical devices.

The transition into flight came without a learning curve or much effort by me. It just happened at some point during my travels on this planet. I eagerly took to my new reality as a flying being. I still had a physical body as did most of the people who flew without wings.

The spirits moved too fast for the physical beings to see what they were up to and what they were. Or how they managed to move so quickly around us. I wondered if they had rapidly moving wings similar to hummingbirds. And whether or not they had a type of physical body or if they were strictly spirit beings. Questions that eventually resolved themselves as I trudged through this queer reality.

MASSIVE CREATURES ROAMED THE PLANET

It may sound like hyperbole, but it is not. Towering creatures larger and higher than multistoried buildings traversed the landscape of this planet. The creatures had their "own" time zones and located in vast harbors covering thousands of acres adjacent to large cities and large bodies of water. The creatures were capable of flying, walking, hovering, crawling, swimming (cruising the oceans and seas), and morphing into other types of creatures in the dinosaur category and beyond that category. The beasts gorged on humongous trees and other types of unique and exotic plant life native to the planet. From ground level on that planet, I was able to appreciate the magnitude of these large animals, if "animal" was the correct terminology for what they were.

I wanted an up close look at one of the large creatures so that I could get a better understanding of what they were and how they operated. They roamed the land as did dinosaurs but were many times larger than dinosaurs. I hopped a tram that took me near enough to place me in walking distance of the beasts; this had taken place before I learned to fly or before I knew I could fly, or I simply forgot that I could fly. I walked right up to one of its massive stumps (feet) which covered a good amount of land. This creature had four humongous legs that were larger than some of the colossal buildings in the city.

I looked up at one of the creatures from ground level and saw it from a flea's perspective. Compared to that large creature I was no more than a flea.

Like a flea, I climbed up on one of the feet and then the leg of the beast and inspected a few of the massive crevasses notched into its tough leathery looking skin. Critters lived in the wrinkles of skin and fed on parasites living on the skin of the monstrosity of a beast.

I was immune to the aggravations of biting insects that swarmed around the massive creature, who apparently was not immune to their torments. The beast grunted and scratched at the insidious insects, to little avail. Stifling heat and bitter cold in different parts of the planet, and in different levels of this big animal didn't bother me either.

The highly bizarre flora and fauna, and creepy-as-hell insects, and other inhospitable bugs and critters that made up the ecology of this planet would have been extremely hostile for mortal beings such as humans. Human bodies were not designed to handle the extreme temperatures and the pressure variations of this planet, or much of anything else that roamed the land. The wildlife and critters didn't seem harmful to us dead people, but I would not want to be anywhere near some of the animals roaming free if I was in a human meat body.

Some of the large and bizarre creatures had wings and the ability to fly off the planet and were able to travel to other planets and moons within the star system. The flying creatures were not impeded by a need to breathe the air while off the planet and flying through space. The beasts did breathe, but they seemed to be mechanical as much as animal (if not all mechanical).

For a better gander at the flying creature, I flew alongside one of the beasts that were in flight and looked right into one of its large dark eyes. It was totally aware of me and looked right back at me. It was a soul-wrenching experience being so near that huge and potentially belligerent thing. Not that it could hurt me since I was already deceased.

It was a strange feeling being so up and near to something that amounted to the size of a large city and flying through the sky as easily as a small bird. The flying city (the beast) seemed to be alive and acknowledged my presence, and existence.

Until then I wasn't sure if the large creatures were animal or mechanical. I discovered during my interaction with that thing that there wasn't any difference between animal and mechanical and that all living things animals and humans are sophisticated hardware and software contraptions. Some animals have souls, human souls, and some humans have souls more inclined with soulless animals.

When I looked into the eye of that large flying creature, I saw apparatus performing a whirlwind of activity. I saw a solitary human soul attached to the machinery that gave the creature life and awareness. The eyes in the body I was in had the ability to see human souls intuitively. Souls looked like colorful orbs. I was not yet at a level to understand the implications of machines fused to human souls; whether machines were slaves to the souls or the souls the slaves to the machines. It was information far above my paygrade. I knew that Earth was soon to cross that bridge as synthetic based technology caught up with the biologically based technology and merged at some point.

The creature (ship) or whatever it was, was traveling to a nearby moon that was twice the size of Earth's moon. I saw large openings, windows on the big large bird (ship/creature) and what looked like feathers covering parts of fuselage/body, of the metallic thing. I flew towards the hull of the ship and found myself inside of it. I had passed through one of the openings, windows without glass.

Inside the innards of the bird, I saw a city that could accommodate multiple thousands of people. It was a huge city with buildings, streets, sidewalks, parks, lakes, and a wooded area. Undaunted by the craziness of it all, I casually flew down to one of the many outdoor cafés in the heart of the city. Seemed like the normal thing to do, and I sat down at one of the available tables; so strange, so otherworldly! So Alice in Wonderland!

I didn't know what to make of it. But I did know that strange was all the rage, and the games played in the afterworld. Rationality had no power and didn't exist here. Everything was possible no matter how cracked it would seem back on Earth; it was no wonder so many souls newly released from insane-asylum-Earth remained glued to their security blankets, teddy bears, and pacifiers. Remnants of insecurities from one type of craziness as exist on Earth didn't have a smooth transition to the mother-of-all-craziness in the hereafter. This place took some time to sink in.

While sitting at the table at the cafe, I could feel and see the wispy beings waffling around me and coming and going as they had been since I entered this planet of the strange. There was no escaping the swirling fairies even inside the bellies of the flying beasts. I was unsure if the pixies would modify their behavior inside the bowels of this creature, which offered up a far different reality and atmosphere than what was outside of it. It was an alternate dimension with far more paranormal elements crammed inside the creature. It was a world like that of a Russian nesting doll, realities within realities.

Bizarre objects swirled around the place changing shape, colors, and sounds. Kind of like being inside a fish aquarium with multiple types of exotic fish and other sea life swimming around. The wisps seemed to move slower, and some of them did stop for a moment and talked with me. They got into my mind and rummaged through stuff like in an old closet satiated and full of junk. Junk that was lodged tightly in there and brought things out and to my attention/awareness. I was eager for a bit of the scoop concerning this place, but all they did was scoop out stuff within me that I wasn't ready to receive. I wanted them to provide me with insider information about this bizarre new reality I was nearly choking on, gorging myself on. A reality

I was forever locked inside of, and only received a smile and a giggle or two before they flew off at lighting speeds.

Before entering the beast, none of the Pixies took the bait of my dogged invites to stop buzzing around me and hobnob instead. I knew they could hear my thoughts and requests, and I made plenty of them. I wanted to hear their thoughts and opinions of my unrelenting pestering for additional tantalizing information. I had been spoiled like a child in a candy store and wanted all the candy, NOW! I'm surprised they didn't throw me out of the big flying bird and put me on a one way ride back to Earth.

I learned soon enough that it was my needling that summoned them to come around me as if I were a screaming baby at a nursery in need of attention. They had been subtly working on me from the moment I arrived, but my state of euphoric confusion didn't allow for me to take full notice.

As soon as I sat down at the table (inside of the beast), a waitress came over and took my order. It was a female-looking robot. With human qualities that were so perfect that a real human could never pull off looking so human. That was my clue that she wasn't human. She was gorgeous and so polite that it made me melt into my seat and left me speechless. In addition to her good looks and charming personality, beautiful gadgets and things flew around her and made her all the more mesmerizing to be near.

The polite humanoid handed me a menu and asked what I wished to drink if anything. My momentary loss of concentration snapped back, and I asked for a moment to collect myself while I looked over the wine menu. I was still leery about drinking and eating for the fact that why eat and drink if you don't have to eat and drink? I didn't even crave food and drink. Nevertheless, I was delighted to engage and indulge in all the mysterious wonders this place demanded I try. I ordered a glass of white wine and soon realized I had an insatiable craving for wine. I then perused the food menu with the enthusiasm of a child in a toy store. My mood about food had changed rapidly once the menu made its entrance in front of me.

The menu was on a tablet-type device and my mind scrolled through endless and mind-boggling food choices. One item on the menu caught my eye immediately. Dinosaur steak? I just had to order the dinosaur steak! There was a picture of each entree and it looked like a T-rex. Mind-boggling, to say the least. There were other dinosaurs and far more exotic animals on the menu to chose. Many were in the appetizer category like dinosaur egg soufflé and deep-fried dinosaur strips and all kinds of strange sounding versions of Raptor marinades, loin-of-lion, etc. I ordered a sampler plate of the appetizers and was looking forward to the main meal: a juicy and tender steak of raptor! A red or burgundy wine might have been a better and more suitable choice.

The wine, the meal, the atmosphere and the view, from the inside of a large flying creature, was spectacular at the very least.

It would be easy and cheesy to say the dinosaur tasted like chicken, being they both are of the feathered lineage of the fowl family, but the dinosaur didn't taste anything like chicken. T-rex tasted powerfully tender for such a terrorizing animal residing at the top of the food chain and boasted a tangy tinge of frightful flavor to it.

The flying city/creature had transparent skin that was terrifyingly see-through (had I been human and suffered acrophobia). It was as if there was nothing between us and the outside of the big bird. Fear of heights was strangely still in the back of my mind even though I could fly and never again die.

I could see the whole outside world from inside of the bird, the mountains, the cities below and those above the skies too. The rainforests, streams, and magnificent waterfalls were breathtaking postcard-perfect visual delights and made up much of the landscape. All the while I was sitting in a truly exotic café' and sipping on a glass of wine that was fit for the gods! Gods who had yet to reach these cosmic heights of awareness where this bird and this planet resided.

The transparency of the bird was not apparent when I was outside of the bird and flying next to it before it swallowed me. Who on Earth would believe such things possible even in their most preposterous dreams? It was all real and beyond fantastic here in the land where the dead know best how to thrive.

We of the dead are alive more so than the people on Earth could ever hope to be while alive. And as one of the dead, I could care less about what the people on Earth would or could believe. Not a very pure thought or comment on my part, especially from me, who spent much of my life on earth as a certified conformist to the popular and mainstream beliefs; and chuckled along with others when talk turned to the paranormal and what I once admittedly called the supernatural, poppycock.

Ironically, I was one of those human skeptics walking around with blinders so thick it was a wonder I didn't trip and break my delusional neck. I was proud of my ignorance and sometimes flaunted my obliviousness during the worst of my ego-driven lives for a good portion of my existence. Good thing for me the universe didn't take offense at my intense and pervasive moronic stupidity!

My body needed no food or drink and was designed to exist indefinitely in this world without such frivolities, but food and drink supplied much of the enjoyment that I was experiencing on this planet. The body I was inside of was beyond fantastic and allowed for extreme appreciation and enjoyment of food and drink. Eatables which were unlike any foods found in fabulous restaurants that I dined at back on Earth existed everywhere on this plane of existence and in abundance.

The lack of aftereffects of the wine and the food too was the best part. On Earth when I overindulged on a fine wine or a delicious meal, I had to pay dearly for it with a hangover and indigestion, soon after or the day after. The body I had now metabolized the food and drink completely without the need for digestion, elimination or a hangover.

It wasn't long before I began to see other people in my level of awareness. I saw them more clearly. So much more than when I first arrived and believed myself to have possessed perfect vision. These were not the masses of people I first became aware of after leaving the office building with my guide. Those people were on many different levels, and all of them, and me too were scurrying around trying to make sense of our new reality from diverse viewpoints. Eventually, each of us was funneled to our perspective places that were more suited to our awareness levels.

Awareness was in constant flux but when a certain level attained, reached, that person entered a new dimension of reality and was around people nearer to their levels, even when in the same city or place with all the other people and their different levels of consciousness. But I only saw the people at or near my level; the rest were like ghosts. I and my kindred-level spirits were apparitions to those on lower and different levels from us.

A few people on my level of reality became visible to me while I was at the café enjoying my steak and wine and the marvelous sights and sounds caressing my soul. I wasn't sure if the people coming into view were the wisps that had slowed down and became physical like me, solidified. Or if they were always there and I had entered their level while I was enjoying my marvelous dinner.

I learned it wasn't the wisps but people I had caught up to and was somewhat on the same vibe as them. That was one of the quandaries of this rabbit hole, filled with playful bunnies leading us on a trail of mind games and adventures through a maze of fun and playful challenges.

There was no correlation or order to the flow of time and the flow of information with the flow of people, which tended just to happen at a perfect moment. Things could show up and then vanish and replaced with other bizarre situations. An acid trip was more predictable and less fluid. I have never done acid, but one of the guys in my office back on Earth did and often talked about his very strange trips on the drug.

It was a random and curious world that we of this place existed. But it had a strange logic and order to it, and it all did make perfect sense after each situation unfolded and presented itself; in a big picture kind of way. Certainly inexplicable in the three-dimensional stream of reality, as things flowed on Earth. Things certainly don't flow that way up here in the land of multiple dimensions. Humans on Earth flow so slow that they appear nearly frozen in time, in comparison.

After finishing my T-rex raptor steak for the umpteenth time. And enjoying it over and over again while savoring a second glass of the godly wine, for more times that I could keep track of, I noticed, even more, people populating tables nearby and doing the same as I was doing. Extending their pleasures over and over again. I didn't know what they were eating, but they seemed to be enjoying it as much as I was enjoying my meal. Now and then someone raised a glass of wine as a toast to someone else or other, who did likewise and then returned to their extended focus on their heavenly dish of good eats.

The wine did not intoxicate the mind at all, which remained clear as a bell, and I could have drunk as much wine as I wanted without getting drunk or getting up for a pee. I did drink a lot of wine at that one sitting. Heck, life here was intoxicating enough without any wine or substances that expanded the mind and the belly, but the wine tasted so good!

Back on Earth, I didn't drink much and never became drunk during my last and final life. I avoided drugs and stayed away from anything that might alter my senses to any significant degree (most of the time). Which was not my reality in many of my other lives on Earth. Where getting drunk on beer and wine before, during and after battles and raids on hapless villages was very much a part of my preferred way of living life.

I became aware that I was repeating over and over again the things I loved and enjoyed doing. I had been doing that all along but was mostly unaware of it. Tiring of things was an earthly phenomenon and certainly not a reality on this plane of existence. Like children on a playground doing the same things over and over again simply for the enjoyment of it; while the parents and teachers on the playground were bored out of their minds.

The people that appeared out of nowhere at the café were humanoid as I was and were no different in appearance and mannerisms than humans were back on Earth. The people went about their business and kept to themselves as I was also doing, and paying little if any attention to me as I tried not to pay much attention to them. Something was different about their appearances, which for some reason didn't jump out at me or hit me until some time later (the people were all naked). After I had become aware of that, I tried not to stare and appear out of place. Many people sat alone at their tables, as did I; a few had others sitting at the tables with them.

I learned that the single people and the couples, friends and their associates (or whoever), were as I was, fairly new to the cosmic wonderland. They were at or near my vibrational level, and that was the main reason I could see them and not see them. They fazed in and out of my view because we were not exactly on the same wavelength, not tuned in completely, like picking up a radio station on the dials of an old radio. We, people like me, seemed to ebb and flow depending on where on the dial we were from each other. It didn't matter because everyone was content with their frequency levels and many of us were slowly drifting up the cosmic radio dial without knowing it.

My lack of dialog with others had nothing to do with being shy or unfriendly. I simply had no desire to approach anyone and ask if they had recently died. It didn't seem like an appropriate ice-breaker to me. I could have talked about the wonderful and perfect weather we were having inside the innards of a beast that we were flying around inside of, but I didn't. It all seemed so normal and natural in the land of the wickedly paranormal, where the dead were infinitely more alive than the living back on Earth, and having the time of our lives.

There was no tab to pay and no money in my pockets if there were a tab to pay. I didn't have pockets I had to keep reminding myself. I was nude! If I were dreaming, I would be feeling uncomfortable and looking for something to cover myself up with, as I always did during that kind of dreams. Not here, I hardly noticed that I was

66

without clothing. I didn't feel a draft and was immensely comfortable, so I was ok with it. Not that it was my choice. I had no choice in my attire whatsoever.

I got up and walked down one of the streets to check out the rest of the town. The Android, who had served my meal, didn't chase after me to demand money from me and instead tipped her hat as to wish me adieu. And yes, she was naked too, except for her hat. I only noticed she was in the nude after I got up to leave.

It would have been normal back on Earth to pinch myself to see if I were only dreaming but I had no doubt that I was not dreaming. Besides, nothing on this marvelous new body I was in, hurt. Pinching myself would have accomplished nothing at all, for I was incapable of feeling any pain.

As on Earth, there were streets filled with every shop imaginable, not to mention, shops that I could never have imagined in a million years. Mostly quaint restaurants and entertainment venues and some strange places that I had no allures or desires to explore further beyond the storefront window.

Music and song were big inside that big bird, seemed to be a lot of concert halls in that town. Singers and musicians could be heard bellowing out sweet and entertaining melodies that covered every conceivable taste in music.

I could see the musicians and they were of the mechanical sort, human-like but not human. Single people milled around, and populated tables in many of the eating establishments and the music halls, all of them stark naked. I speculated that most of them knew they had no clothes on. No one seemed to care. Those other beings, the invisible ones, due to their higher rate of existence and experience, moved at such high speeds that only a blur of them registered in the mind. And they continued to race by me without slowing down to communicate why they were in such a big hurry. A few did stop and talk, not that I can remember what they said. I remembered some aspects of their faces but not enough to recognize them. Didn't see their bodies so I had no idea if they were nude.

I wasn't sure why I wanted to talk with the fast moving souls and not so much to the souls traveling in the slow lane with me. I was more curious and fascinated about the movers and shakers that rapidly buzzed by me, more so than the ordinary folks like myself who appeared distant and uninterested in talking. That made me want to pick up my pace of progress through this maze and catch up with the highflyers.

While walking by one of the many establishments on that stretch of road I was on, a strange old tune emanating from one of the shops caught my ear and wouldn't let go of it; like my mother did when I was a young lad and didn't listen to one of her demands.

I entered the building that the sound streamed out from and sat at a table near the stage to hear more of it. On stage was a quartet of musicians, all robotic, playing bongos and drums and strumming some strings to the tune that had caught my ear. I hadn't heard that sound in many ages, several lifetimes ago. I ordered a bizarre drink that popped into my mind after being stirred up by that intriguing sound, but I could hardly pronounce the name of the drink. The drink was also a memory from a time long past. The Android took my order without asking me further details about the strange brew and quickly delivered the drink to my table as if it had been premade and was waiting for me. It was a bitter tasting coffee-like concoction that I drank at some obscure place back on Earth and or on Mars. I wasn't sure; I was having difficulty remembering the place as if I had tried vigorously to drowned-out that memory at some point in my murky past existence.

I became grossly mesmerized by the hypnotizing music and got lost in the droning and sickly melody. Soon my mind expelled a stream of ancient memories that had lodged deeply into the crevices of my mind so many centuries ago. I became aware of past lives that the guide skipped over during my life review when he shared many of my past life memories with me. Apparently, life reviews don't tell or show the whole sordid story of all past lives.

I was a slave on another planet, Mars. Our village captured and conquered by a race of strange beings that had ravaged, terrorized and menaced our planet for many millennia past and present. Much of the surface cities laid waste, by the intruders, and most of the survivors moved to other planets by them, and the rest of my people migrated (hid) below ground. Mars had a large population that lived in underground cities before the attacks, but much of that population was rooted out and exterminated. That was ancient history, and I was one of the Martians that was born and grew up underground many centuries later.

After capturing us, the beings drugged us and loaded the whole village onto a large spaceship. One of many ships that came down to the planet to cart Martians away as they had been doing for endless epochs. The trapping and capture of Martians had been a practice far before I was born on Mars, and which continued unabated to present times. Over the centuries, we were rendered into a primitive people and were defenseless against these highly advanced race of beings. We feared the strange "gods" with their powerful flying machines that often came down from the sky and plundered our cities and enslaved many generations or Martians.

Once on the ships, the drugs they fed us kept us in a drug induced state of confusion and a state of drowsy sleep. We remained that way for long and extended periods of time. We were hibernating, but no one could know for how long our sleep lasted. I remember waking up every once in a while only to be given more of the drug to keep me drowsy and asleep. Sometimes the drug didn't knock me out completely, and I could recall the long intervals of storage subjected on us. Others in the tribe/village experienced similar breaks in consciousness, waking up and then being put back to sleep as I had been, by the mysterious beings or their drones.

That coffee I was now enjoying was the drug given to us before our long sleep. The drug didn't have any effect on me now other than to awaken deeply embedded memories. The music was the droning sounds inside of the container ships. Madding at the time but now the sounds were only sweet memories of a horrible time in my life.

At some prescribed period, the ship carrying us inside of it like caged animals, for a duration no one knew or could understand, and parked above planet Earth (we didn't know that at the time), released its cargo (my village).

We were taken down to the planet in saucer-type ships and reestablished in northern parts of Earth, where temperatures were more in line with what we were used to on Mars. So as not to suffer additional shocks to our physical bodies and minds, on top of what we had already suffered.

Rumors that our community was hybridized by our leaders, with the humans on Earth, and that most of us had our minds wiped clean and then filled with new information about the planet prevailed for a time. Such alien notions soon lost their meaning in our community as we acclimated to Earth's environment and barbaric ways over the centuries. There had been many Martians brought to Earth hundreds and thousands of years before my village. I was one of the men placed into a leadership position after settling on Earth.

After a considerable amount of time had passed, we believed ourselves just another race of humans, not that anyone gave those kinds of ideas about coming from Mars, much thought, other than some of the shaman turned leaders, who sometimes talked about planets and star systems. And then often ended up dying in battles or accidents, to keep that information from propagating. Humanoid beings like those that transported us to Earth also became leaders who ruled over the many villages settled on Earth.

When we first arrived on Earth, the concoctions of brew mixed with other additives were continued to be provided to the people in the village. To further induce permanent amnesia by wiping away lingering memories that might have survived the drugs/coffee concoctions that became a staple during our cold storage in space.

We were required, forced, to build shelters and training centers, and numerous other types of facilities for the warfare that we were trained and instructed to partake in.

Copulation with humans to increase populations for armies was encouraged and enforced by our leaders. Raiding human settlements and killing men and boys, and taking females to breed with, was the primary objective of the vigorous training we Vikings undertook, soon after coming to Earth.

Raiding and pillaging human camps by Viking clans destroyed a viral breed of human hybrids, a mixture of renegade beings that mated with humans and flourished after the destruction of the Roman Empire, which was carried out by some of the same renegade clans. The renegade hybrids from other planets in other star systems was a viral menace that penetrated and quickly spread rapidly across Europe. Similar menaces also introduced plagues and other diseases carried from space onto the planet Earth, which stretched across many periods of time.

Such maladies contributed to widespread famine across the planet, for lack of humans toiling in the land to produce crops, due to the high death tolls. Viking raids combined with natural mayhem was a kind of cleansing operation for crop rotation for various humanoids that would call Earth their home. It was a process that this planet went through periodically by the order of cosmic protocol, instituted by the local gods in charge of planet Earth, who sometimes allowed viruses to penetrate into Earth and plague the planet.

I remember our Viking raids so clearly and feel a sense of shame come over me. We brutalized and eliminated many farming communities situated near rivers, streams and coastal towns that were easy prey for us. We impregnated the women and slaughtered all the males that we could find and catch so that they could not impregnate women and compete with us.

We sometimes ate our enemies, bones and all. Pulverizing the bones for the marrow and mixing it with other foods. We did it to spread fear in the villages that we intended to annihilate. It was genocide on a large scale over several hybrid races that had infected the Earth. We took their belongings, their gold, cattle, and all their livestock and then burned and destroyed what we could not carry and take with us. We sold many of the women into slavery to other Viking clans and other nations that we traded goods with, for gold and silver. The bounty, the prize, allowed us by our elusive masters.

I died in a battle during a raid on a village and was buried unceremoniously in a pit with the rest of my murderous crew; by the town's people that were victorious over us. My brutality caused me to suffer reprisals in numerous other lifetimes that I was condemned to live during several epochs on Earth. It was forced reincarnation even though we provided a service to those who had brought us to Earth, from Mars.

I paid my awful dues in sweat, blood and tears over long periods of time afterward, losing many of my children during various lifetimes at the hands of tyrants like myself. I learned through repeated anguish the real value of a human life, and the terrible cost of feasting on the labors of others, which ultimately came with a very high price.

As Vikings, we serve a purpose prescribe by our masters, so a few of us received a chance to make amends for our actions. Not all men who did as we did receive opportunities for redemption from their wicked deeds. Such men remain in the pits of Hades for crimes committed with glee, and returned to the cosmic dough from where they originally came. There they will spend time until regenerated again and given opportunities once more to prove the value of their true nature if any.

I feel blessed and have no painful remorse, having my crimes commuted by lofty karmic retributions and cosmic impunity. I am truly grateful that only one ounce of good in me was enough to clear my soul and spared me from further damnation. I and a few others did our jobs but took no pleasure or glory in watching others suffer, during our tumultuous raids on numerous human villages.

The horrid tasting potion that I drank on the spaceship so long ago and that kept us in a zombie state of mind, tasted far different now and had a more pleasant aftertaste. I drank it down while in a pub located in the belly of a monstrous flying bird on its way to a fabulous resort on one of the several moons of the paradise I now call home.

I took my last swallow of the poisonous, evil, potion that I was now immune to, got up, and flew out of the city through the nose of the flying beast. Had no desire to stir up additional convoluted memories that were buried deep inside the belly of the beast, at least for the time being. I was satisfied and at peace with the sordid memories as they would forever be a part of me while I existed in this universe. Redemption is truly a cosmic gift that few souls as I deserved to receive. But most who diligently seek it, find it.

STRANGE AND WONDERFUL PLANET

While I was on Earth, my mind could hardly grasp the enormity of the universe. My personal universe, my everyday mundane needs and wants, boggled my mind, let alone the ideas of a vast and never-ending, cosmic universe. Which remains, even at my higher level of understanding, difficult concepts to grasp.

While alive on Earth, my thinking abilities were normal, and I was mostly confused about things that shaped our human lives, like religion, politics, science, space and nearly everything else. We humans lived on the same planet, yet it seemed everyone had different perspectives and ideas about everything. Few people were ever on the same page of understanding the mysteries of life and plagued by the constant disagreements and arguments over the basic values we all shared. It seemed that people were more interested in themselves and less interested in facilitating the achievements of others.

This place was different, and I could feel that many of the invisible spirits whirling by me, were imparting information to me that was helping me along my path to higher places and higher understanding.

Cities on this planet, most of them, were beyond futuristic in design and atmosphere and resided in the fairytale province. Cities were manicured and perfectly landscaped with monstrously high buildings that connected the surface to the stratosphere thousands of miles up in space and anchored deeply under the surface down to the very core of the planet. Fabulous structures each with their own peculiar and unique personalities that flourished and swayed with the multitudes of people attracted to them in some cosmic ballet. I wasn't quite yet ready for the dance floor and stayed on the sidelines a little longer.

I flew up into the sky above the large creatures and the tops of the cityscapes and gawked at the diversity of structures all over the planet, and all of them were oozing and radiating people, a most peculiar sight to take in. Superstructures, both natural and constructed by machines, often one blending in with the others, mountains, beasts and mega-cities, enough to titillate all the senses inside of my temporary body. And there were far more senses than what humans have on Earth, in their bodies. Which I hesitate to describe not wanting to sound like a deviant, to juvenile three-dimensional minds.

I swam through the air like a bird in flight, enjoying the freedom and the wind blowing through my hair without the work of wings, but with the work of nearly invisible spirits who diligently kept me afloat.

The knowing that it is not the wind (ego) that keeps you afloat but the love of other beings that clears a path for you to move ever higher is unparalleled.

I found my delight in the afterworld; it was the gift of flight, and the appreciation of the love I received that kept my soul energized. I flew through the cities and towns and enjoyed the sites of Greek and Romanesque architecture (things that I enjoyed is what mostly came my way), slowing down only to capture details in the narrow corridors of each and every city that I visited. Other cities boasted other types of architecture some that I have never seen before in my thousands of previous lifetimes, and that were equally mind-numbingly delightful places to experience; and savor, for the first time and every single time after the first time, which numbers boggle the mind.

Some of the people (spirits) on the planet remained a blur to me still. There was a lot of "soul" movement at speeds and frequencies much higher than the frequency I traveled. Even with my ability to fly rapidly through the skies, spirits passed me as if I was standing still. I had a physical body that kept me from breaking through some barriers and into the spirit whirlwind, where few who entered ever returned.

I was picking up speed and becoming a blur to many of the new arrivals to the planet. Most of them remained more focused on themselves, until being hit by the shockwave of the new reality that was slapping them silly and knocking the air out of their strides. My physical body was still undergoing changes, a transition, and a metamorphosis of sorts, with the help of the spirits.

I never felt alone because I was never alone. I was on a constant high, due to all the positive vibes imparted to me by the mostly shy beings; but very present beings in my life. And those visitors were growing in numbers. My spirit became freer and abler as the numbers of spirits increased around me. Every moment with them took me further and deeper into the spirit realm and each level that I breached took acquiescing. I couldn't imagine things becoming more enjoyable than they already were, as I acclimated to the cosmic wonderland from one transition to the next. But I somehow knew I hadn't yet tasted but a single grape in a large vineyard that was overflowing with ripe, juicy and sweet grapes. The vineyard beckoned all the souls who entered this planetary star system, to feast on the abundance of marvels created exclusively for each of us. What a massive undertaking it was by the beings running the show.

Things on Earth were never "crystal clear" as they are here and now, and becoming clearer all the time. I have escaped my contradicting existence as a human being and am finally destined never to return to that empty shell of human existence. My mind is born anew, of the things I have acclimated to since my death and my passage here from Earth. There is no confusion even in the fact that so much remains to be explored and adjusted too. I have a sense of comfort in my mind and body like was never possible or achievable as a human on Earth, in any of my lives.

Awestruck at every moment. "How could that be?" I thought to myself. As a human, it required drugs and alcohol to keep the buzz going for a few minutes, and that only lasted for short durations. And the buzz eventually turned into body pain, headaches, and depression, and sometimes was followed by despair. I hardly ever, if ever, fell into the drug trap on Earth but some of my friends in school and at work did.

"How generous can the universe be for departed souls such as me? And will this feeling of peace, tranquility and joy last forever?" I asked in my mind expecting an answer. The answer came, and "forever", is what it said. Spoiled in the short time I came to be truly alive, soon after I died. I wasn't sure how much time had passed if any time did since I arrived. I was not aware of time or need to be anywhere or do anything. On Earth, I would be considered a bum or a billionaire socialite to have such scandalous freedoms as I have now.

My funeral popped into my mind, and I chose to go to it. My parents and a few friends from my office attended. My parents grieved, and my mother sobbed. Uncles and aunts were absent. I was never close to my uncles and aunts, and neither were my parents. Most of them lived out of town so it was no surprise that they didn't or couldn't make it to my funeral.

I could "hear" the thoughts of all the people at the funeral. Not garbled but clear as a bell from each of the twenty-six people in attendance. Apparently I had made a good impression on all of them, therefore, spared from any hateful, and negative thoughts that might have emanated from them had it been otherwise. Surprising to me, all the people there had love in their hearts towards me, even those I believed were jerks and didn't like me. I must have been a nice guy to be around. I did try but was never sure how people viewed me.

I decided to depart the funeral before it was over, not wanting to see my grieving parents suffer any longer. Soon after I left I received a message in my mind that their guides would remove most of their grief by subtly letting them know, I was doing just fine in the dead zone. That made me very happy. You can stack happy on top of joy in the place I am now; how crazy is that?

I had hardly scratched the surface of this new reality that consumed me. Every possibility brought giddy feelings of anticipation. Every moment was a holiday laden with surprises and presents. I didn't even know where to begin my adventures, and yet I was having the grandest time of my existence so far, and only three days had passed on Earth, since my abrupt death and absence from that place.

But the three days was no indication of the time that had passed on Earth, or where I was now because I was able to see my parents ten years after my funeral, in what only seemed like moments after seeing them at my funeral, and them living happily on Earth.

Such quirks of cosmic strangeness persisted and presented an unremitting mystery about the many wonders of the universe and how and why they unfolded so vicariously. Gratefully, mysteries had a way of dissolving away and resolving in my mind as my awareness increased in short segments, and sometimes in leaps and bounds.

The star system I was in was an excitingly busy place. Objects of every shape, size and color filled the skies and space between the dozens of planets and moons in that star system. Souls on many levels shared space with each other but seemingly were unable to communicate freely with each other. But it was only my limited perspective as one of the freshly minted people, and I didn't know the true nature of communication between souls, only what I understood about communication from an earthly perspective, and my experiences while in this place.

As things progressed, I saw more people like me entering the large sphere of the star system (as I had done when I first arrive). They had similar bodies like mine and seemed to be lost too; in their own unique and absolute amazed ways.

Early in the stage of this game, soon after arrival, it was best not to have the distractions of casual conversation with other strangers, who were just as green and lost but filled with overwhelming astonishment. Not that anyone on this plane of existence was considered strangers. Everyone passing through the gates to this place was good quality people, or they couldn't be here. Casual conversations seemed impossible, if not rude. It would be like talking in a theater when people were fully captivated by the movie on the big screen, and trying to focus on that alone, rather than on the other theater patrons whispering or talking in the background.

I wasn't ready to have conversations with others of my pay grade, and the feeling apparently was mutual since no one came up to me for a talk about the captivating wonderland.

I flew towards the massive and exhilarating star that teased us from its high perch far above the planet. The planet revolved rapidly around the sun, much faster than Earth moved around the sun. It was exhilarating for those allowed on this planet, and it was like a fast moving Disney Land ride. The rapid movement around the star would have made a human from Earth very dizzy, sick and dead, in that order.

The disc of the sun took up much of the sky and made for a superb visual sight for those privileged to see it up close. I could look directly at the star without any effect on my supernatural eyes, body or mind.

As I neared the star, it grew and became colossal. I was an insignificant speck on the face of the blazing gargantuan star. Waves of energy blasted by me and through me and would have vaporized me long before the point I had reached, had I been inside of a human body. I stopped and gazed at the raging torrents of plasmatic tentacles leaping furiously past me as if I was standing before a blast furnace with the force of millions of nuclear bombs. All I felt was indescribable exhilaration rolling over me, and blasting me with pure joy. The experience added tremendous new knowledge to my ever expanding reality. Some things can't be described or shared only experienced.

The star is huge and could swallow hundreds of stars the size of Earth's sun. The star is life to all the planets and moons in its sphere of influence. Trees, plants and the wildlife on the planets and moons were nourished by the magical rays of the star, as is true with all the star systems giving and supporting life throughout the galaxy. It was surprising to me that this star operated similarly to Earth's star. But Earth's star was a drop in the bucket compared to this star. And this star did so much more than the average stars in the galaxy. This star entertained spirits that were destined to rule large portions of the galaxy's hundreds of millions of star systems. It was totally mind-boggling and humbling to be a part of that reality!

The afterlife was on the same plane of existence as was the life on Earth, dimensionally speaking. The body I was inside of was not controlled or nourished by this star, as my body on Earth depended on the life-giving force of Earth's star. My new body consisted of a different form of energy than what emanated from stars in this dimension. Nevertheless, stars have multiple dimensional properties, and I wasn't sure if entering the star would have any effect on my mind, body or soul.

I entered the star and was spit out. I don't know if it happened immediately or if I had been allowed to rummage around inside the star before being rejected. I was not ready to know those things at this point and would try again when my vibrational levels increased further, and my knowledge base more substantial. I wasn't disappointed or offended that the star rejected my soul and body, and understood that receiving information and entry into certain forbidden places only came about when the soul was ready for a transformation to happen within the soul, and not a moment sooner.

I explored other planets and moons in that star system and was fascinated by the simple wonders each planet and moon offered up to visitors like me. Similar but less astounding wonders exist on Earth, for the enjoyment of the human inhabitants, too. But such wonders on Earth can only be fully appreciated by the lucky few people able to travel to far away and exotic places, where the natural beauty existed unless they happened to live there or nearby. The best things seemed always to be far away and scattered around the planet, where most people could never go to or experience except through pictures, books, and movies.

Additionally, such fortunate humans who have the ability to travel are still restricted by mortal bodies that can be injured, killed, fall ill or worse, and become bored. Such limitations placed a damper on real enjoyment. I can enjoy all the thrills without the damaging effects of the spills. I go fishing in the most spectacular rivers, streams and lakes without the bustling crowds, pesky insects or restrictive weather that ultimately ends up taking the fun out of fun. Becoming bored up here is totally preposterous. Such words don't even exist in these realms.

I am not in the biblical heaven, not that there is such a place or thing, but I can't imagine this place being less than heaven times a million. I mountain climb for the exhilaration of the climb, ski down snow-covered hills so terrifyingly steep that I would never have imagined doing so on Earth, in my last life, where I wasn't very adventurous. Being like Superman makes everything worth living for, and not dying or becoming damaged-for.

Pushing the limits by the avid daredevil on Earth has no redeemable qualities other than the fun extracted from the thrills and spills. Brownie points are not handed out by higher beings for having fun in the face of danger. The reward is whatever the person can squeeze out of whatever it is they did or do for the adventure or experience of it.

Learning is one element achieved by pushing the limits of endurance on places like Earth; which is true for every achievement humans manage to snag out of the Jaws of Life. The experience is the reward. Regardless of the gamble, the danger, the heartache, the brutal perseverance and the "perceived" selflessness of the endeavor or act. All such actions, heroic or whatever, accomplished by any individual are ultimately for the benefit of that individual "alone"; even when other people are involved and saved by such heroic actions. Hero worship and the pursuit of heroics are the biggest delusions on Earth and are nothing more than pomp and subtle ego trips and traps.

All work is carried out and performed flawlessly by machines and other types of living paranormal devices designed to cater to our every need and desires. Machines that look and act as if they are alive and happy to be of invaluable service to the transitional physical beings on this planet. Machines serve around-the-clock. A clock that I have yet to see since coming to this place. Clocks, Timepieces, watches or any other gadgets and devices that tell people the time of day are not needed here and don't exist on this planet or realm.

Day and night have no meaning here, being that it is practically daylight all the time. No one on this planet or in this star system ever sleeps. Far too much going on and no one needs sleep. There are places, zones that qualify as nightspots with dark skies and all the corresponding lustrous stars that are unlike any starry nights on Earth.

Such places are inside of buildings with synthetic tapestries and props to imitate the nighttime atmosphere and making it far more tantalizing than the real thing. It is a production for the newer physical beings still in need of some nightlife and star-wonder in their lives. Many underground nightspots fulfill that restless craving that was adapted by humans long ago while on Earth. During the time before recorded history, where humans often lived in terror under the night skies and looked up to the sky for sorely needed solace.

Such artificial wonders held cosmic memories for the humans placed into isolation on training planets, where survival of the fittest wasn't a slogan but a very real reality. Shining stars in night skies are the mementos for isolated souls away from the cosmic delights that beckon the souls return. Nightspots on this planet are popular for the physical beings in transition mode, who still yearn for the wonder and comfort of starlit nights, the very things they now have right in front of them but are not yet fully aware of that reality.

I considered myself being on the first or second rung of a celestial ladder that reached to the stars, and to all of the adventures found in those mysterious starry places. There are few height restrictions for moving upward after breaching the gates of this place. It's amazing just how many people are too fearful of entering the gates to this place and chose instead to return to Earth or other similar hiding places, to continue in the lives they are comfortable living.

Most of the restrictions and reservations that I had run across during my early stages here, soon faded away and turned into opportunities for grasping more of the things that continued unfolding around me. Every new revelation brought additional pleasure to my soul.

From where I am, which changes from moment to moment, the pinnacle of existence and higher realization and understanding, is achieved by the simple act of enjoying the process. Which to a lesser degree is also true in the game of life back on Earth.

Far too few people have grasped the concept that the increase of knowledge is fun and rewarding. I was never one of the smart kids at school, and I struggled a lot in the learning arena back on Earth. Because for me, learning was hard work and required too much study time after school and little desire on my part to do it. Not here in this place, where knowledge is bestowed on the people at every turn and free for the taking, like at a parade where some of the floats throw out candy to the eager children lining the streets. Learning here in pre-utopia (for some) comes without any real effort on the part of those who wholeheartedly partake in receiving the gifts tossed out to them. Just thinking about the endless possibilities for souls that have reached this summit of the knowledge Mountain, gave me goosebumps, or would have, had I been still wrapped inside of the human skin.

Where I am is not where everyone that comes to this corner of the universe is. Some people come in much higher than I was at my entry point, concerning awareness of the things of this universe. Those souls quickly leave the slower souls in the cosmic dust, as they blast right past us and enter the ever-richer realms in the exclusive world of the spirit beings. Many of them will move into utopia planets and places, from here, and live in their new environments for as long as they deem necessary.

At the other end of the spectrum, there are humans that come here for short durations before falling back down to earth, for various reasons. Their lack of achieving sufficient escape velocity to break free of the strong gravitational karmic forces, keeps many held down like lead balloons. Some souls are fearful of change, and the more rapid the change, the more they fear it, and simply refuse to move forward. Those are the souls that had chosen to return to Earth and provided with similar lives to what they had before they died.

Some souls can stay out of the lower realms they escaped from and had no fear of moving forward but choose to go back to help loved ones left behind on Earth. But most souls that miss the boat due to their baggage of dirty laundry have to go back to continue their reincarnation cycles until that baggage falls away from them. Such souls come here to this planet for a short pep talk and a brief life review before being sent back from where they came. Depending on their particular status and circumstances determines how much of this paradise they are allowed to see (but not explore) from the lobby, before being placed back on the turnip truck and returned to Earth.

I was allowed to sit in on a few review sessions of the souls that were destined for a return trip to Earth. I remained out of view of the souls undergoing a reaming, during their life reviews. Many were in shock that their lives and activities merited so little. They believed themselves kind, gentle and loving towards their fellow man, and their pets, mostly their pets. And some of them believed they were doing good things to help the world, the planet, and never realizing that they were doing things that made them feel good, for the sake of feeling good; which is the only reward. Recycled their trash and cleaning up the dog poop when taking Fido for a walk was not enough to break the chains of the reincarnation cycle when the soul festered and hemorrhaged with hate, ego and envy.

Religious people as a group were far more incredulous that they could be sent back to Earth when they didn't even believe in the silly notions of the reincarnation blabber. Some of the souls pointed out that their holy books promised eternal salvation, guaranteed by faith alone, and not the deeds of individual souls. They had become convinced that a scapegoat named Satan was the root of the evil in their souls, and therefore, they shouldn't be held accountable for anything.

So many such souls have fallen for similar scams and deceptions on Earth, and so many such souls are returned to earth kicking and screaming. Few of them find religion after they are returned to Earth, having been scarred in a previous life and having little appetite for fraudsters. And some begin to realize that they have to take responsibility for "all" of their actions and dirty deeds against their fellow humans.

The souls that make it to this star system for reviews were souls with fewer defects than the general population on the Earth and other such places and were likely near to become full-fledged citizens of the spirit realms or physical realms in utopia. Perhaps requiring only one or two more lifetimes on planets such as Earth, to clear up minor discrepancies and to do more work on their juvenile and naive beliefs.

Souls with any rap-sheet don't make it to this star system and are sent to other places for reviews, followed with little if any respite in between their hellish lives.

I was asked if I wanted the job of reviewing souls that came here for a peek of the afterlife before they were sent back home to Earth. I politely wiggled my way out of it. Unsure if that cost me future privileges or whether I lost brownie points for my first job refusal.

My life here hadn't changed meaningfully shortly after that refusal, and I took that to mean that I dodged a cosmic bullet. Retribution seemed to have a life of its own in this universe, and one could never know if they had crossed that fine line in the sands of time, and had to duck for cover. However, retribution was mostly reserved for souls on Earth-type planet, which was all the more reason for those souls to get busy and figure out why life on Earth isn't all fun and games. Up here, everything is fun and games regardless of what, if any, responsibilities, people chose to engage.

I felt unqualified in the area of sending people back to Earth. I couldn't do on to others what I wouldn't do to myself. My soul ached when I saw people break down, pleading not to be returned to Earth. I was fresh off that bandwagon Earth, myself, and could not imagine being sent back for "any" reason. Therefore, I couldn't justify sending people back to that hellhole. That was my reasoning for not taking the job. The job required a thicker skin than what I had at that time. My skin did thicken up as my knowledge base thicken up (increased). Ironically, that happened "only" after I shed my "skin" and became all spirit.

Earth, with all its beauty and majesty, is a place of torment, pain, suffering, wars, hate and a bastion of ignorance. And few people can escape any of those plagues for any length of time while on Earth. Not an easy place to achieve spiritual growth.

Souls who received their reviews on this level, and were destined to return to where they hailed from, were given choices on where they would be born and what they would encounter and face during their next life on Earth. Race, sex, occupation, country, and religion, were some of the choices they could choose. Most souls reviewed at lower places than this place had few choices if any, to pick from, and were often placed in conditions recommended by their guides, which was sometimes a harsher environment than their previous lives.

Personal guides tended to have tough and thick skin, which came with a side of horrible negotiating skills. When representing the people they monitored from birth to the grave guides were like drill sergeants and didn't cut anyone much slack. They were not sympathetic listeners either, concerning the souls, they looked after (The humans who often pleaded to them for advice, mercy, and special privileges). Guides have a clear and unobstructed view of the things humans are capable of doing during their everyday lives. Guides have heard every excuse and sob-story a billion times and therefore are hardened. People who were making attempts not to be jerks had far better reception and positive responses from their soul guides.

At the level that I have reached, I could go back to Earth if I so desired, and be on vacation and do fun stuff all the time (live and be one of the rich and famous). The kind of dream-life that most people on Earth envy and end up despising those who have it. Such deriding fools simply don't understand the dynamics of how things work in this very generous universe. Vindictive and jealous behaviors are common mistakes and traps that snare so many people on Earth, who then end up missing out on the enjoyment that is all around for anyone to partake.

Most of the good things that Earth has to offer are left on the vine to rot, by people who are too busy hating and envying others instead of going out and harvesting their crop of good fortune.

I would have no requirements placed on me unless I chose to make my vacation a working vacation. Souls that escape Earth can choose to take a chance and go back in blindfolded in order to test their resilience further. Those who do usually have little trouble and end up sliding through life as if they knew what they were doing (which they do). Once goodness is in the soul, it stays there and can't be lost or nudge loose easily.

Some souls do go back to Earth, perhaps because they enjoyed Earth's harshness and challenges; and living on the edge of madness. Such brave souls usually take on leadership positions as kings, queens, presidents, superstars or any number of wealthy and famous celebrities or corporate moguls. But they are mostly souls sent down and employed by higher spirit-beings to perform certain jobs on Earth, as humans.

I had no sexual feelings or desires for intimacy in my new heavenly body. Unlike the sexual feelings that drove me up the wall when I was a human, and went without resolution much of the time, being that I was too shy to act on my urges. I dated a few women but never developed a lasting relationship with any of them (in my last incarnation). I was somewhat insecure around women, which made me and them uncomfortable. Soon after puberty, intimacy was something I struggled with all of my life. In high school, most of my friends had girlfriends and were sexually active with them. They bragged about it and made fun of me for doing without a girl. My sexuality questioned by both the girls and boys in my small circle of friends. I was heterosexual, and a bit intimidated by girls, more than I was willing to admit to myself and others. Therefore, I spent many lonely nights while my friends had all the fun.

I don't have them kind of drawbacks now that I'm dead and rid of my human flesh and its flaws and anxieties. Apparently being weak in those areas of my life didn't hinder my ability to advance out of the Earth zoo. Which as far as I was concerned was quite an achievement for me, considering my wretched lives of centuries past; where I recklessly and brazenly indulged in sexual escapades and barbaric behavior at every opportunity I could muster.

New arrivals happened continuously and arrived as if they were on some gigantic conveyor belt and dropped off onto this cosmic processing star system. One can only imagine the huge numbers of souls in the Milky Way galaxy alone; which is in the endless trillions. And the souls that reach maturity and the required escape velocity from their resident planets every second is enormous.

There are numerous star systems in operation throughout the galaxy that perform similar functions like this one, that act as transfer stations for souls that are moving up and out of this realm and into the higher regions of existence all over the universe. Most galaxies serve in some capacity, as soul-handling machines. Processing souls that have been coated in flesh and held together with skin and bones, and then slow cooked and flailed until they transformed back to the spirit world.

My body had all the sexual equipment, and presumably, it all worked. Male genitalia wasn't pronounced as it was on Earth, in a human body. Up here and in this body it folded up out of view and out of mind. Females had typical breasts as back on Earth, and they were out in the open. I haven't had the opportunity to experience sex and didn't know what it would be like in these higher level places. But the thought had crossed my mind as I began to notice more and more single women showing up in places that I frequented. It was very strange when people seemingly appeared as if they were beamed on to this planet out of thin air, as if in some Star Trek movie.

Souls swarmed onto this planet in continuous waves and deposited by the thousands with each wave hitting the shore. Once on shore, they materialized anywhere in the metropolis. When and where in the metro was determined by their level of skills and knowledge they possessed at their moment of entry.

Some souls bypassed their guides and escorts at the gate as if they already knew the ropes and were already familiar with this place. They had clearance to enter freely, having traveled through here in their dream-state before they had died.

Souls were reviewed in several locations inside the city and most were turned loose soon after, while others sent back to Earth. Many souls lingered awhile in special places hidden from the rest of the people before they made appearances in their new physical bodies. The great majority of souls that landed here bypassed the physical bodies altogether and went straight through to spiritualized zones, cosmic lands, utopias and other destinations of their choosing.

Many spirits did linger and took pleasure being around the allegorical caterpillars in their physical bodies that were not yet ready to cocoon up and burst forth with spiritual wings.

I was a caterpillar for a duration of time, feeding and feasting on the vast flora and fauna in stark abundance in this Garden of Eden. Fattening myself up so that I too could build my cocoon of knowledge and then burst forth and take flight into the next phase of existence.

Souls washing ashore in untold numbers still came ashore alone and not with groups of souls, regardless if they died with others. When multiple casualties take place, such as wars, natural disasters, and accidents, where souls are related and have died together, they are treated and processed individually, as are all people that die and sent to the appropriate places for handling based on purity level of their souls.

Married couples don't arrive together unless they are going to the same place, which was rare (but they could meet up later at some point). Friends and family did come to these shores together but were in the minority. If they were able to recognize each other and made attempts to communicate; most could only because they were on the same trajectory. High flyers who were more aware of things than the average newcomer, flowed directly to magnificent lounges where they could hang out with others, friends, family, and associates, who were already here.

Children, when they came to this place were taken young from Earth because they were ripe and ready to move up the cosmic ladder, a trajectory mostly earned from a previous life. Souls of the young bypassed the physical bodies like the one I was in and became part of the swirling fast moving and nearly invisible beings that flew right past the rest of us, like warm summer breezes.

I have not had significant casual contact with people on this planet, other than being nearby, sitting at a table at a restaurant, or riding on the tram or another mode of transportation with them. I enjoyed walking around the cities and watching other people's reactions to this incredible new reality. I could feel their warm radiance without making eye contact or being up close and in their faces.

Far more desirable was the contact from the souls that whizzed by and for a moment flirted, before disappearing too soon into the abyss of the mist as if they were the shy ones. Stealthy beings were a steady occurrence and at times an overwhelmingly euphoric manifestation that rattled the minds of the souls they stopped and communicated with.

The solid body, the apparel that was currently clothing my soul, was a way of easing the mind away from the physical and towards the spirit existence. Humans have spent eternities existing in physical bodies during their many lifetimes on physical planets as Earth, and the weaning process from such ingrained realities begins after they break free from physical worlds, and begin their migration to the spirit realms. That transition can be a long process for some souls and a short process for others.

SINGING CITIES

Large massive cities glowed and sparkled and sang strange soothing songs, continuously, which created an atmosphere of magnificent sights and sounds. Every city acted as beacons, beckoning people to come and take part of the splendor within them. Drawn by the enticement, I flew to one of the thousands of such cities and spent a little while in each of them, the ones that I could relate. Cities were everywhere, suspended in the skies, covering much of the landmass, on and "under" the seas and oceans, and the whole of the honeycombed interior of the planet.

The space above the planets and moons harbored several large spheres and massive cubed cities. Many of them were linked together, and I could penetrate some, but others I could not enter. Those I could not enter had nothing in them that I required for soul growth and therefore pointless for my transformation process.

The cities were designed to cater to physical beings who were slow to grasp the essentials for forward momentum. Spirit beings invaded and saturated the cities to help the momentum along by swarming around the physical beings like sheep dogs. The nature and purpose of the interactions between the physical and spirited beings were complex and individualized. Everyone that fell into those cities had differing needs and requirements, and the spirit beings helped in filling out the necessary paperwork for them (allegorically speaking).

The many dimensions people navigated through made things perplexing for those who lingered in the physical form past their time to move along. Often such people were swarmed with the magical spirits that brought focus to the slower ones so they would continue on their road to ever more bizarre realities.

Every physical being here was on their personal path/destinations to the spirit realms as in a grand central station. Spirit realms that were as diverse and as plentiful as the grains of sand on endless beaches. Realms are as unique as snowflakes sprouting into existence across the universe. Being able to transcend mystical and multiple realities and dimensions were exhilarating but also jarring to the mind and soul, and sometimes a kind of pushback happened. Questioning the progress of other people slowed my progress.

The cities were marvelous places with shimmering interior walls, with large curved structures, humming with tunes that ebbed and flowed. From the innermost parts of the planet below the surface, and up to the very tops that protruded into space, like massive bellowing pipe organs.

I wasn't a religious person, but some of what I witnessed in the city reminded me of the grand cathedrals I saw while traveling to Europe, as a child. I was on vacation with my parents at the age of 15, and not very interested in the magnificent architecture at the time, but the sights did make an impression on me. Not like here and now, "impression" would be a colossal understatement.

Thousands upon thousands of people were clinging to the concaved and twisting spirals as if glued to the walls. But they were not stuck to the walls and people came and left in a constant swirl of activity. I went up to one of the walls and embraced the wall to see what it was all about. So beautiful, soothing and intimate as if the buildings were alive and they embraced you back. Many mysteries resolved themselves while on the walls. Pleasant to the touch it was difficult to pull away from the structures.

After spending unknown quantities of time sampling many of the colorful walls I detached and floated towards the top. As I moved up, I observed tens of thousands of people going to the walls in every direction, staying only for a moment or an eternity. And then as I did, release the wall and float upwards. Contact was as exhilarating as river rafting off a canyon of the soul, twisting and turning while enjoying magnificent views of things ahead and all around.

After reaching the top, which was several miles above the ground below. And like a circular infinity waterfall, millions of people spilled out over the edge and spread out in every direction. Thousands of similar towering stacks oozed streams of people flowing in and then out and into space.

Like a child at a Disney Land ride, I flew down to the bottom of the structure and did it over again, and again, and then trying other structures, never tiring of the cosmic thrills each ride delivered. Every tower was a unique experience, and I could easily see myself doing this for eternity if it was allowed. There were endless millions of such unique and hugely diverse pleasure-palaces impregnating the planet.

After spending the equivalent of days, weeks, months, perhaps years, there was no way of knowing how long I was engaged in that peculiar activity, due to the irrelevancy of time, a spirit came and loosened me, pulled me free and sent me on my way to a much higher reality.

Time was so damn irrelevant that no one on this planet paid attention when they became consumed in activities that bogged them down like children at play. No one was hampered by time which was a blessing and a distraction in its peculiar way.

Time was such a burden on Earth. I was always concerned about time, controlled by time, consumed by time. There was never enough time to do the things I thought important. Now everything is important and all the time in the universe to indulge important stuff was in abundance. It was very important to enjoy the things one wanted to make them happen and burst to life.

ORIGIN OF SOULS

I was never more at peace as I was now, on this titillating planet. It is quite the contrast from my physical existence that reached back millions and billions of Earth years, where I spent many of my lives wallowing in misery and ignorance. It was a long arduous and torturous road to get to where I am now, where I have reached this point of my existence, and to relish my refined reality.

I began life in another star system hundreds of light years from the star system that created planet Earth. I learned that my essence existed forever, and even before I came to be whatever it is I am now. My soul-substance was in a much different formulation than now.

My soul was not born on Earth or inside the sun as many humans believe. It was a dormant creation that came to bloom like a flower out of the soil on a warm spring day after a long winter's sleep. Then lingered for a while sopping up the rays of the sun, before dropping off the stem and becoming one with the dirt once more.

From the cosmic dirt, I began my long, treacherous existence as a mortal being and will once again drop my physical body back to the ground where it originated. And leaving my spirit to ascend, take flight, and soar forever to unimaginable heights like a seed riding the cosmic winds.

Many methods for soul activation are used and employed throughout the universe. Some souls came to be, like waves in the oceans in a perpetual gyration of the exotic spiritual matter. Souls then are activated and come into existence in cosmic sprays. Soul-matter created by generative spirits at the higher realms with nothing better to do. Then spawned onto an ever-expanding celestial swirl of increasing awareness and sentience.

Souls are then harvested from the waves and collected, separated and seeded into special star systems, where they are further processed and separated once more, into batches. Some batches of souls move up into the cosmic void, without further processing and serve the universe in various ways from the void, for specific needs and requirements designed by the higher sources of beings behind the curtains of existence.

Other batches of souls are processed further in the furnaces of life on the surfaces of stellar spawn, the many planets that serve as repositories of endless creations seeded into distant star systems in distant galaxies. Certain handpicked souls receive further cultivation and undergo intense distillation to purify them to the extreme, for a greater purpose in the cosmic order.

Human souls come from a branch of souls that number in the billions and are a caste of a far different order, which will serve a sector of galaxies far different than what humans are aware. Human souls are souls forged on hellish planets over the course of countless lifetimes and separated like wheat from the chaff (good souls from the defective souls). The bad souls, the chaff, are disposed of or used for other purposes around the selected galaxies for dirty deeds. High-quality souls have the universe as their own to do as they wish.

As soon as souls attain freedom from the cosmic machinery that churns out endless types of souls for the numerous purposes and the vast requirements that keep the universe humming, they remain free forever and can never return to the cycle of labor, from where they originated.

SPIRITUALIZED

As understanding increases the physical body fades away and increasingly spiritualizes. I came to realize that my ability to fly was part of my expanding awareness that accumulated on my soul. The energy and enlightenment imparted to me by the partly invisible beings that whirled passed me and around me created more freedom in my soul and helped me enter a higher vibrational level of understanding. I was becoming invisible to the newbies that were flooding into this star system and onto to this planet, the people recently placed into physical bodies and moving at slower vibrational speeds.

I was catching up to the faster swirling invisible beings and began to phase into some of their higher realities and join with them. I recognized them slowly and one at a time at first, until the numbers rapidly increased. We didn't speak words with each other but somehow we knew each other's thoughts, backgrounds and the many past relationships we shared in past lives. Details about them poured into my mind whenever one of them came near me.

A shipmate from hundreds of thousands of year ago on Mars, who I saved when the ship, during a battle, sank into an ocean that is now long gone. A mother, who gave birth to me and then died soon after. I was a woman, and the property of a man who shared me with his soldier-friends, and who ended up killing me during a drunken brawl. It was a short relationship, a very horrible and painful one for me. That same man ended up being one of my children in other lives as well as being one of my wives (possessions) through the ages of time. A daughter of mine in one of my happier lives, and I ended up cherishing more than life itself. At some point, I became her grandchild and died young. That broke her heart, but now I see her as a man again, a brother, who I got along with exceptionally well.

I was learning the many bizarre faces of this existence. Brothers, sisters, fathers, friends, acquaintances and my offspring that numbered in the endless thousands, millions, as far back as the birth of the star systems from where I, and they began our long and often violent journeys and relationships. Our life long bonds forged in the shedding of blood, abuse, fierce hatred, forgiveness and love, concern and comradery. We became harder than steel that was melted down and reformed into our spirit family of souls.

My family of souls was around me all along, throughout my endless numbers of lives. Those souls that I touched in some positive ways ended up helping me along my difficult journeys through the rough waters of life, as I did for them during my life and while residing in the in between lives zone.

Souls deserving of receiving extended vacation time between lives were able to reach back into life and help those they loved. Such interactions have kept the lifeline intact and strong between family, friends, associates and adversaries. The strong bonds crafted over many lifetimes made it possible to be eventually pulled out of life's difficulties and placed into the cosmic realms where friendships and relationships revealed themselves for what they are, forever enduring.

Souls that have survived and thrived by goodwill and deeds, and the help and encouragement from other souls in their circle, are providing assistance to like-minded souls, on planets similar to Earth, all over the galaxy and the universe.

FRAGMENTS OF PAST LIVES

My mind wondered from the present to the past. Past lives, any of them I could retrieve as if they were a file on a computer hard drive, and explore them in detail– simultaneously with other things I was doing now.

Some of my past lives were fun, adventurous and productive, and a few, all of the above during the same life. Most of my lives were a mixture of both good and bad things I did to others and that others had done to me, so we were even. Only if it worked that way, which most times it doesn't. Far too many of my other earlier lives in various parts of this universe were barbaric, hateful and downright scary. Even in my deeply depraved soul there was always a small flickering flame of civility that reaped a sliver of warmth for my spirit. Enough to keep the seeds of decency alive in my soul and give it a chance to flourish and thrive, which it did. Otherwise, I would not be here in this place.

Gratefully, I had paid for those sins in previous lives, and they were not hindering my progress to the spirit realms significantly now. But the stains remained and are a constant reminder of my horrific past. However, such discrepancies in myself allowed me to be more sympathetic and more understanding of others that had gummed up their souls in similar ways and behaviors. And that is an agreeable tradeoff in my book.

GRADUATION INTO THE COSMOS   LOU BALDIN

PAST LIVES HIDDEN IN DREAMS

My body dead below me, a dark void and then light. Calm and peace beyond my wildest dreams. I see no one but feel the presence of many. Soothing silence as I move towards streams and waves of living and intense colored light. I transcend the cosmos and enter a realm distant from physical, cosmic space, passing through layers of countless dimensions. I arrive and am engulfed by the light but no people, no souls of family, friends or supreme beings, waiting for me.

I feel only indescribable joy inside of the light but only for a brief moment. I have no corporal body to weigh me down, and I float or glide at tremendous speeds towards the unknown. I feel as if I have a body with the extremities, arms, legs and head. I feel as I did when I was alive minus any pain or fatigue. I have no control of my movement through the light but am aware of the shadows of dying souls whirling by me.

I come to a stop and surrounded by Brick buildings. "Am I back on Earth?" I think to myself. They are not familiar, but it appears as if they belong to a city on earth. They don't, I'm on some distant planet in another star system. Hundreds of brick buildings five or six stories tall, dozens of them. Many are half demolished, and it looks like an urban renewal project is underway.

124

A person is with me; I know him, but he is not from Earth. He is younger than me, by how much I didn't know. I don't know how old I was. I feel young about thirty or forty years old. I was much older when I died, in my fifties. The buildings, abandoned, empty. No people in the streets only my companion and myself. We walk into one of the buildings and go through each of the rooms as if we are looking for something. My companion finds a box of papers in one of the desks in one of the mostly abandoned rooms. We look through the papers and find obscure meaning in them (nothing that I can understand). We leave the papers on the desk and go through other rooms in the building where we find documents with my name on them. This place was a hospital, at one time and I was a doctor in the hospital. My companion was one of my patients. I don't recall the details because I don't want to.

We are outside the building, inside of a car, my companion, the patient, is driving. I don't think to ask him where we are going, somehow knowing where we are going. To another building. Much of the town looked forsaken, but in the distance, I notice some activity. We abandon the car and walk through a deserted street. It gives me the creeps, knowing that danger always lurks in rundown parts of town. My companion and I somehow became separated, and I continue down the street towards the activity. I walked into what looked like an underground garage and noticed a group of shady looking men, standing around. A dead man lies nearby on the dirt floor. Looks as if recently beaten to death. Blood had pooled around his head and midsection; shot in the head, and his whole body looked badly beaten.

One man is sitting at a desk and giving orders to the men standing around, who looked unconcerned about the dead man lying there near them. The man at the desk sends some of the men off to a job site. He looks up and at me and asks me if I'm looking for work? I told him I wasn't. But he convinced me to go to the job site with two of the other men that were standing around. I go with them to the job site. Once there I reiterate to the two men that I wasn't interested in working for that man or with them. By that time the boss man, the man at the desk, comes around, and I tell him, I'm not interested in doing any work for him. He told me it was not up for discussion, and that I now worked for him, "like it or not," he said.

The two men I went there with, turned on me after he gave them the nod, and mercilessly beat the crap out of me. Damaged one of my eyes and busted a rib or two, then they tagged me like I was an animal, with some strange device that kept me from escaping. The next day I was at the job site working at one of the abandoned buildings, hauling bricks in a wheelbarrow, cleaning the mortar off the bricks and stacking them in a pile.

It was dirty and hard work, and I didn't feel well from the beating I received the day before. I had been at the job site for so long that time had lost all meaning for me. I knew I was dreaming, but I couldn't wake up. I dreaded every start of the new day and hardly had a restful sleep. My injuries and sore muscles from hauling bricks all day long, wouldn't let me. I felt like I had been there for a month, perhaps much longer, an eternity. One night I fell into a deep sleep from the sheer exhaustion of my broken body and damaged mind. And I dreamed I was dead, the dead man I saw on the ground when I first got to this dilapidated building, in this hellish place. The man at the desk, the boss man, was my former patient, who had participated in beating me to death.

I'm dead again, and I'm off to another city, country, planet, galaxy, I had no idea. I enter a vibrant place full of life and happiness. I'm gliding like a bird through beautiful streets and canals. I ask my invisible companion about this wonderful place. Was I on earth or some other planet? It was another planet, she said.

Believing I'm in a dream I look intently at every detail so that I can remember parts of the dream when I wake up from the dream. My companion slows down so that I can get a better look at the surroundings, then tells me I'm not dreaming. It's a modern city with colorful storefronts and fascinating architectural designs.

Populated by humanoids but not humans as on earth. I was resting before my next life; she told me. Then everything went dark. I had entered a new body, a newborn baby on another world.

Another life in another dream

As the Vietcong (VC) made their approach towards our camp, we waited, like men on death row, believing that it would be over for us soon. Recon advised us that several enemy battalions were about to engage us. The first claymores exploded indicating the breach of our perimeter, about several hundred yards away, minutes later more claymores were triggered. VC were now a few hundred yards from our foxholes. I was positioned behind a machinegun and drenched in sweat from the fear and the horrible heat of the noon sun. The humidity was cooking my brain. Insects were buzzing all around, and I can't keep them away. Insects inside of the foxhole were crawling everywhere. Insects crawled into my boots and up my pant legs. I removed my shirt because of the heat and rolled up my pants to keep them from soaking up water that had collected in the foxhole. It rained earlier that morning and turned parts of our camp into a mud fest. I bailed water out of my mud hole with my steel pot (army helmet). Until Charlie (VC) demanded all my focus be on them.

Charlie was marching on us like army ants on steroids, and they would soon overrun the camp by their sheer numbers surrounding us.

The nightmare came alive, hundreds of Viet Cong permeated out of the jungle, and we opened fire on everything that moved. My machine gun was steaming from the hundred percent humidity coming in contact with the hot-as-hell rounds flying out the barrel like fireflies from Hades.

Torrents of casings filled the air as quantities of bullets streamed out the barrel and ripped through trees, brush, flesh and bone, of the Viet Cong soldiers advancing on our position.

From the sky came choppers dropping off American soldiers and were flanked by a batch of attack cobras looking as menacing as a horde of biblical locus unloading fire and brimstone on the VC.

The choppers deposited squads of infantry on our position, which increasing the chances of our survival by a few notches. Which meant doom for the peasant soldiers charging us from every direction.

Rather than turn and run the Viet Cong kept coming at us. Throngs of Viet Cong advanced over the mutilated bodies of fallen comrades and showed little regard for their individual lives as if they were high on drugs. Some of them were barely armed, advancing on our positions with bare hands, bamboo spears and rusty bayonets on their dilapidated rifles.

I looked at some of the faces of the men I killed, mostly teens, but many looked old, in their fifties or more. As I gazed upon the stench of death that lay before me, I was gripped with unceasing horror, not only from fear but also from the realization that I had become an instrument of death! After hours of fighting the shooting abruptly stopped, and everyone held their breath wondering if it would start up again. It didn't and night approached, and men remained in their foxholes and consumed C-rations in the dark. Flashlights kept off so as not to give away positions to the enemy.

I had no appetite, and could not find peace in my mind from the bloodbath of that day, and more to come at daybreak, if not sooner. The god awful screams in the dark of night from the wounded sickened me. I was alone in my dark foxhole, except for the insects and the many other creatures that scurried around in the dark of night. I pulled the pin on one of my grenades and held the grenade in my hand and up next to my chest. The explosion destroyed my upper body, and shattered my beating heart, and I was dead.

I woke up from the nightmare in a sweat, and I was trembling. I was not a soldier in my last life, and I didn't serve in Vietnam. But that dream was not a dream, the soldier that blew himself up was my patient, the one who had beaten me to death for a perceived crime he believed I had done to him in a previous life. I was able to see and experienced his final moments of life on Earth as if I was behind the machine gun with him. Technically, it was as if I committed suicide the same moment he did. I knew and felt every tortured moment as if I were him.

Something squared up between us in his moment of despair and insanity. I was able to move on from that shared past entanglement with him. He had other entanglements with other people still to deal with, and his soul was moved instantly back to Earth and placed into a baby's body in the jungles of Vietnam. As a baby girl, a daughter of one of the Viet Cong he killed that day.

My patient, Mitch, from a previous life, had committed suicide. His name as the soldier in Vietnam was Chuck, and his name as the boss-man that had murdered me in a previous life was Jay. Three different life intersections with that soul and nothing worthwhile developed between us. Mitch and I would never connect again in the physical or spirit realms. Not all souls mesh and get along, and end up going on different paths and be with souls more suitable for them. If I wanted to pursue additional life situation, with Mitch, I had the option to do so. Mitch didn't have that option. And I chose not to.

The dream world is a world of past lives. But only shards, clips of things that happened in faraway places and during other time periods, and shown, regurgitated in a place of higher dimensions in the mind, sometimes inside a magical ship, and therefore, difficult to understand. People also dream of things in their current lives, where sometimes they work on problems and find resolutions.

I was still alive in my last life and safe in my bed when my mind vomited out bits of memories of other lifetimes during dreams. I experienced a slew of dreams months before by car accident. I didn't connect the flurry of dreams to anything other than I had a bunch of dreams. But my guides were busy preparing me for this afterlife, behind the scenes. And I had no idea, no premonition, hunch, or omen that it was going down.

The clarity was astounding; it was as if I was reliving cherished moments of my childhood. Things and situation that puzzled me in the past became clear and less mysterious. When I was about six or seven years old, I remember seeing many balls of light and had always wondered what they were. Now I know those same balls of light are things I saw while traveling from a distant solar system at a rapid rate of speed while inside of a strange metallic vehicle. That vehicle pulsated with images and sounds that took me places in my past lives and the in-between places between lives. I was inside of a UFO, that thing I never believed existed. During the voyage, a voice described were I was going and why. When I awoke the next morning that part of the dream, as I had believed it was only a dream, was missing. My mind was wiped clean of the memory. I later discovered that I was summoned by higher beings and taken to them and given information concerning my life.

I was never interested in astronomy in school although I learned a little about the planets in elementary school, which was the extent of my knowledge of the universe. I was not attracted to science fiction books, movies or television shows. I never realized that there were so many stars systems until I was much older but didn't care that much about astronomy.

As my journey continued, star systems rushed by like raindrops on the windshield and an overwhelming sadness came over me. In the distance, I saw the star system in which I was going to. It became increasingly larger as I approached. The ship slowed down, and I could see the planets flying by, one by one, in a matter of minutes, not days, weeks, months or years, not even hours. The sight of each planet was an incredibly emotional experience for me as if I had seen them many times before (which I had but was made to forget). The dread I felt intensified as I was now entering a new nightmare, a new lifetime. A life where I was destined to be a doctor.

Dreams are seldom in the order they occurred in real life. Which dreams appear at any given time depends on what triggers the dream. Life situations that are karma driven are what usually trigger a certain dream or dreams. Plucking the dreams right out of the subconscious mind where past life memories can be hiding or from an extraterrestrial encounter aboard a UFO ship.

Previous to being a doctor during the Nineteen-hundreds, I was a doctor, a medicine man, with a native Indian tribe hundreds of years earlier. In that life, I was descended from Vikings (my ancestors which I was one of my ancestors) that had journeyed to North America and encountered hostile native tribes. Imagine that; we were bred to be the hostile ones that few could out maneuver. Having killed off and displaced numerous peoples in Europe.

We Vikings took people by surprise but in this strange new land, we were taken by surprise. Shortly after we arrived battles ensued and eventually worn down as our numbers decreased with each encounter with the natives. My clan of Vikings lost contact with our village in the land of ice, and consequently, we were unable to regroup and recruit additional fighting men. Still, we managed to survive a few years before succumbing completely to the Indian raids on our camp. Survivors of our clan were taken into the Indian village and over time allowed to become part of the Indian tribe.

The food was plentiful in the new land, and the tribe grew, swelled and prospered. The tribe became large, and the leaders decided that it should split into smaller tribes, groups. One tribe turned into three tribes, and each tribe went off on separate paths. The tribes claimed ground near rivers and streams and for a time didn't compete, and peace maintained. There was more than enough food for all. And we feasted on the bounty of the land. Turkeys, geese, ducks, deer, hogs, rabbits, moose and fish, and anything else we chose to catch and eat. We only moved our camps to get out of the way when melting snow and heavy rains turned creeks and rivers into raging floods. We lost people during unexpected flooding that washed away teepees and many of our people. The other reason we moved camp periodically was due to the stench that built up after days of accumulated human and animal dung, near and around the camp.

I was chosen to be a medicine man by the chief because of the knowledge I had. I acquired most of my abilities when I was a Viking warrior. I had learned the secrets and the magic inherent in herbs and roots; and had become proficient at mending broken bones, broken flesh and healing mind and body. I healed myself and my fellow Vikings, from injuries sustained during raids and battles; before stumbling onto to this new land. Most of my knowledge came from one of the women we captured during a raid on her village. She was the wife of a doctor, killed during that raid. It took a while before she warmed up to me and shared her medical secrets she learned from her husband. I had planned to make her my wife, but she died during a prolonged cold winter. A year before we made the voyage to the new land.

I died a few years later at the Indian camp from a fatal wound I received from a bear attack. I had taken a squaw as my wife a few years earlier and had two children with her. They were young when I died. My good relations with most of the tribe was due to by my position as a healer. Therefore, my squaw and children managed well after my sudden death.

Soon after my death, my soul was taken by mysterious beings to a dark place. I didn't receive a life review, nor did I interface with helpful guides or meet with family and friends. And then I ended up on a planet that had a hazy red sun in the sky. The sun gave off heat, and the planet had animals and vegetation but not like on Earth. It was twilight all the time. I wasn't there long enough to know if there were seasons as on Earth, but the lack of daytime was very depressing. The moon was missing, and the red sun remained in the sky all the time. The food was strange, but it was edible. Water came from a well in the center of the town. There was no one there to give me instructions, and I simply did what others in the town did.

I wasn't born on that planet; I was dropped off there in a similar body as what I had on Earth. I don't remember when or how I ended up in the body or where the body originated. I saw no children in that town, only adults. The town was not large, and most of the people stayed in their mud huts. A few people could be seen walking around the town, and some people regularly gathered around a campfire that was near the well. Not to talk because few ever did talk, which was more like grunts. People came to drink a mysterious potion, a dark concoction that was heating over the flames of the fire pit, and then returned to their huts.

From my hut, I moseyed over to the fire pit, grabbed one of the metal cups strewn on the ground near the fire pit, scooped out some goo from the caldron and sat on one of the logs around the firepit. I sipped on the hot, dark brew until I became drowsy. I then noticed some food stuff loosely piled near the log circle, and I fetched some of it. And I ate the food while standing there near the pile as a few others were doing. There were no utensils or plates, only our fingers. After eating, I went back for more of the tasty juice. I swallowed two or three more cups of the semi-liquid stuff and then went back to my hut and fell asleep. I began to dream.

My dreams were horrid and tormenting. Many types of beings chased after me and attempted to kill me, do me harm or eat me. The dreams changed before I could be damaged or killed but the fear and the pain were bad enough. I didn't wake up only entered other dreams and continued running from my pursuers. I began to recognize some of the places, and a few of the people in the dreams. Villages we sacked for our masters who brought us to Earth. The people in my dreams wanted to do to me what we Vikings had done to them. But I was protected, and they could not harm me. I was not a good Viking (ruthless killing machine) and shielded some of the villagers when I could, without being seen my other Vikings. I helped some of the villagers escape slaughter. Had I been caught I would have been eaten alive by my Viking mates.

Our raids were horrendous, vicious and often turned into bloodlust orgies. Killing, torturing and raping without restraint. We became possessed as if by repulsive demons. Somehow the carnage began to make me ill. I began to loathe, despise the raids, and my people, who made a living by destroying the lives of others.

There were some villages that harbored strange creatures (people) who were equally horrible and vicious as much, if not more, than we Vikings. They were difficult villages to overtake, as the inhabitants were strong and vile, and made us look tame in comparison. I didn't mind destroying those type of villages.

I woke up from my long sleep and continued the routine on the planet with the red star. Consume the food that was prepared for us and sometimes left in our huts to eat. Sat around the campfire and drank the strange soup also prepared for us. I never saw who made the food or the drink or anyone bringing it to us. There seemed to be nothing to do on this planet but eat, drink and sleep. I did a lot of sleeping and was grateful that all my dreams were not nightmares.

We on that planet, existed in a kind of purgatory, waiting for them, whoever they were, to come and take us away and place us into other lives back on Earth or some other place. I didn't know that back then, but I know it now.

COSMIC RHYME

Winter wonderlands, springtime flowers, and colorful autumn leaves, are the canvases and the gifts from the spirit world for the enjoyment of all conscious beings. Going cosmic to the land where fairies play. Every kind of beings imaginable flit and flirt at work, and the joys that mere mortals fear and stay away. At the speed of light and far, far more, the spirit world gives life eternally. Life to the trees, all the flowers, and the bees, while enjoying the sun filled breeze. Such sprites in the Willow and the cornstalks are all part of the grandness that exists forever, across the lands of timeless dreams, turned realities. Mountains and streams gleam from snowflakes and snow to water that fills the thirst of many things below. From the soil that comes from the plants and the plants that come from the soil, come and go in endless cycles of magic, fed from the spirits of man, shed after dead and then once again all a glow as quick as a gnome it looks down radiantly to the creatures below.

Spirit beings give life and bring life to all that matters in the universe. Spirits are the fire in the sun that heat the planets and create the growth of plants, animals, insects, the workers behind photosynthesis. Humans don't know about the magic they are not privy to, of the enchanted souls that bring to the process of life the physical and nonphysical existence in the cosmic wonderlands.

Butterflies fly and navigate huge distances across the planet and do it with the help of the sun, moon and wind-swept skies. They fly on the backs of magical beings as do ducks, geese, hawks and everything that flutters. Bats sing a tune that bounces off rocks and trees and people too. At night they navigate with the light of the moon and even the sun too, to eat insects and fruit for energy and drop guano as all birds do. To nourish the soil and spread more seeds like Johnny apple seed, used to do. Far and wide such creatures travel performing jobs they know not they have done. Same with spirits who toil day and night and have time to while away in delight. They find joy in keeping things alive and moving so that life on planets by the billions can support the life taken for granted by more than a few.

Spirits are above the gods and are the true and only creators of all living things. Giving life and waking up dormant life put to sleep for future times and reawakened again like dormant flowers looking forward to spring. Spirits never sleep and do their best when everyone else does.

LIFE AS A SPIRIT

No real way to describe spirit life once souls enter and pass through sacred gates that shut tightly behind them. Much of the spirit knowledge is forbidden to fall into the hands of mortals and guarded by spirits of the highest order. Nevertheless, some tidbits as found on these pages are allowed out of the sanctified halls where no flesh or matter of any sort can enter. Not all spirits can go into the hallowed halls unless invited to come in by the supreme of the Superbeings.

Supreme Beings have spotless spirits, having never been marred and blemished by the matrix of matter that exists only by their very command to exist. Supreme Beings have existed in the same spiritualized state forever and can never change. They give life to everything in existence simply by their existence. Their numbers are unknown by all beings but themselves. Their numbers will never increase or decrease. Therefore, no souls can enter into their council, and are forever sealed inside of their incorruptible assembly at the apex of each universe.

Super beings can enter sanctified regions near where the council of Supreme Beings resides; for durations of their choosing. Only select souls know where that place of unequaled grandeur is. Isolated somewhere in the vastness of the never-ending cosmic universe, and tagged in the ever present structure of atoms that serve as a base for cosmic awareness.

I had entered the terrain of Superbeings. Having embraced the process that began shortly after my arrival on the planet, from which I have since moved. And embraced by my cohorts from previous lives who had climbed to the pinnacle of awareness for our types of souls, ages before me. I was not yet a Superbeing, which required other journeys into the cosmic fray. My temporary physical body evaporated and my spirit released into the wondrous halls of celestial purity. I have exited the planet and the star system that prepared me for this profound transformation, and I now resided in a place of true magnificence and grandeur unparalleled in the human imagination.

I was nowhere near being a Superbeing yet but was eternally grateful at having been asked to enter one of the lower exclusive zones, where all souls in the universe yearned to be; which was privilege enough for me.

My exclusive position gave me access to knowledge unavailable to souls not inside of this enclave of near absolute awareness; which was only a shard of the awareness surrounding the Supreme Beings. Nevertheless, the fragment of knowledge granted to me weighed heavy on my soul, and I could hardly imagine bearing the full weight of what the Supreme Beings held inside of their collective wisdom.

"Heavy on my soul," didn't equate to feeling bad, I was in perpetual bliss, and it made me feel guilty, unworthy to have such privileges laid upon me. Feelings of guilt passed quickly, and ecstasy flooded my soul, as I contemplated all the things I could now do and would do in my new position. I had access to massive amounts of material about everything knowable, outside of the conclave of deep knowledge available only to the Supreme Beings.

I learned that the Supreme Beings were not souls and were something unknowable, enigmatic, unfathomable, profound, mysterious, perplexing, confounding, bewildering and impenetrable.

Nevertheless, there was no place in the universe I was exempt from other that the incorruptible council. I could go anywhere and indulge in anything and any activity I wished to indulge in, physical or spirit.

I was above the gods, who shepherded the galaxies and star systems and all the life-forces therein. Gods who often sought me out or others as myself for council, advice, guidance, favors, vengeance and plague, against their perceived or real adversaries. I had the power to give them all that they asked and wished for, without any reservations and any potential repercussions to myself or them, if I so chose to exempt them. That was such mind-boggling power and never fell into the wrong hands, but only used by the spirit beings that have attained to these astronomical levels.

I could allow the gods to take vengeance if I so desired and directed them to do so on my behalf when I believed it judicious and practical. I could and did allow common humans and other similar physical low-caste beings any of their wishes and desires including vengeance and spells they wished placed on others of their caste and status.

Every request came with a price, and I was the one who set the price. Vengeance cost the perpetrators, the requesters, more trouble than the requesters bargained. And invited into their lives much of the same, and additionally, opened doors that brought them more repeated lives. The severity of the plague placed on others and the repercussions and consequences brought on by such requests to the bearer, the initiator of the deeds, brought forth vengeful fruit.

Humans and others of the lower world seldom asked if there was a cost to their hatefulness and treachery against others. And would only discover that there was, during their interviews after they died or sometimes before in their dreams where I talked to them.

Often I met people inside my magical carriages (UFOs); while they remained alive and under the curse of constant scrutiny. I summoned the people or their souls from the worlds they existed on throughout the galaxies and that resided in my domain, and brought them into my presence for a conference. Terror is what they beheld and experienced in my presence. Until or unless I freed them from such horrific restraints.

Knowledge suitable to their understanding I imparted to them. Often to be digested over a period of days, weeks, months and years; depending on their level of acceptance of the information and material I imparted to them. Some people rejected the advice and information and continued in their darkness and madness, having been clueless of where that annoying information originated. Which was their choice to do, and eventually suffer for their continued neglect, with repeated darkness inside of their physical lives and souls.

I scanned the cosmic energy waves where souls in the physical realms placed their desires and prayers to the gods, and where such pleas were heard by other beings with the ability to hear such requests. Beings in the spirit realms of both good and evil. It was a massive field that encompassed segments of the universe inside a cloud of energy, emanating out of massive numbers of souls, from enormous amounts of planets, residing inside of colossal quantities of galaxies.

Multitudes of spirits as myself toiled endlessly in barren fields and tilled, plowed, nurtured and fulfilled the massive wants and needs, crying out to us from inside the soul zones. I retrieved and responded to requests by the hordes of physical beings, who placed desires out there for us fishermen using large fishing nets to haul in for consideration.

We took pleasure in assisting all that we could with the wisdom made available to us, by the Supreme Beings, whose sole bidding we did. All the information that humans and human-type beings across the universe had or received came from angelic spirits, who once were themselves on the receiving end of information for assists to help them through difficult life situations and circumstances.

All higher spirit beings understood and sympathized deeply with the masses of lost souls grappling daily to understand the world they lived in. It was a daunting task fed by the sheer numbers of stubborn souls stuck in their covetous and fearful ways. So many that were eager for relief but not eager to make the changes that brought on the relief.

Some souls were easy learners and were free to enjoy the wonders of the universe after a few difficult lifetimes. Others were in a perpetual self-pity-fest that put them on a downward spiral, unable to see the real problems in their lives as their creations, spawned by their thoughtlessness, and pervasive envious and hate-filled deeds.

Many souls were so deep into their muck that no amount of lives could pull them free of it. Eventually, such derelict and lost souls were sent back to the place of their origin, before they entered the physical realm. After remaining there for what could amount to an eternity they once more were given the chance to trudge through the filth of physical lives. In essence, they were sent back to square one of their existence.

Most souls condemned to the physical realms came in with predetermined packages that stipulated what their lives would be like, with some latitudes added. They saw a few of the hurdles they were to encounter during their trudge through life. Souls knew if they were coming into this life with special privileges and prearranged talents and gifts, as musicians, leaders, craftsman, etc.

When gifts were not part of the packages, some people were allowed to try and develop aptitudes they wished to have and pursue. And if they were successful they would come into their next life with those desired qualities and abilities.

Learned talents were never of the same value as genetically infused gifts from the spirit world. Nevertheless, spirits in my realm could modify original decrees, destinies, fates, fortunes, and outcomes, and allow for changes to such contracts, including lengthening or shortening the time served on Earth.

I knew and had dealings with hundreds of thousands of the souls who were still on Earth, and other planets. Having been affiliated with them through my many lifetimes spent with them. I knew them as offspring, mothers, fathers, friends and associates, and nemeses too. I was now in a position to help them or hinder them. Their progress was in my hands to do as I wished. I could create situations of continued hardship or be merciful and provide them with a life of ease, or stay out of their lives completely. Everything good and bad dished out by me, and others spirits were merited and allowed. Spirits who had advanced to the level of my position had absolute discretion over the souls they chose to assist.

Souls (people) we helped could be helped and hindered by other kindred spirits as well. Souls with evil intent fall victim to wicked souls who happened to be in the area. Evil begets evil, and humans who lean towards evil had many like-minded souls to help them down that slippery slope. Evil souls infest Earth. They are souls who are unable to escape Earth but are allowed to entice humans to join in their squalor and misery. Similarly, people of goodwill are attended by like-minded spirits working with them to bring them prosperity and happiness during their time on Earth.

Evil spirits are allowed to tempt those who lived righteous lives too. Same with those people who are hellbound. Good spirits often intercede on their behalf in hopes that they would see some light, a flicker of potential, in their wretched existence.

Spirit beings came and went in flurries to interact with and be with souls in the physical realms on Earth, and other such places; while at the same time pursuing numerous other adventures and activities of interest to them.

Multitasking is easy at these higher levels of awareness. Spirits could be involved with multitudes of situations concerning souls, both in the physical and spirit worlds, while enjoying endless venues of indulgences anywhere in the cosmos in the same time space.

Many star systems are not training facilities for physical beings. Some star systems are exclusive resort-type pleasure centers for spirit beings. Like at an NCO club on any army base, many stripes and ranks (sergeants and above) drinking at the same waterhole. Pleasures and privileges only are known to the spirits who accepted invitations and engaged in the playfulness of encounters with other spirit beings of similar caliber. Such happenings are the exclusive domain by those spirits that engaged in such activities. Many spirits never leave such places of ceaseless ecstasy, after they discover the ones they enjoy the most.

A portion of humanity lay before me, existing on numerous planets all over my section of the universe. I was aware of so many people but could choose to focus on portions of the star systems in the galaxy; many shepherds (spirits) were watching over many flocks.

I could see to the very interior of people's souls and knew their every thoughts and concern. I knew if they were hateful, deceitful or loving and caring souls or a little of both. I could see humans and others in their daily lives and activities, dressed and naked. Humans had no privacy from the spirit world, whatsoever. Nothing could be hidden from the spirit world. Spirit beings were keenly aware of everything they wished to be aware of, concerning their chosen flocks of people.

I could summon any soul living or dead and have a sit down with them inside one of my many cosmic carriages. I arranged get-togethers for people who lost loved ones and needed encouraging so that they could get on with their lives. I was able to bring to meetings the dead soul regardless of where that soul resided, even dragging them out of Hades for the duration of the meeting if that is where they were hiding. Many souls resisted and didn't want to leave their hiding places. I took them nevertheless. They were a sore sight to see and an awful terror to those human souls who had begged the gods (me) to know about their lost loved ones. Such encounters often silenced those who needed closure and were able to put things in better perspective (once they became aware of the true nature of a loved one's soul), and then put them behind them and live better and more productive lives.

Hades is a place of shame, where souls go when they can't face up to their own glaringly evil past. Excruciating painful it is to see in detail maliciously envious deeds perpetrated on family, friends, and strangers. Souls remain in hideous hiding places for their refusal to enter the process that is required for redemptions to take place. Most are taken against their will to the meetings, where some of the condemned souls regain a bit of insight when they see the people, the suffering souls that they once loved and had left in such dire conditions. Paranormal meetings are beneficial to the lost souls and the requesting souls that take place during "Alien abductions". As spirit encounters are sometimes viewed.

OLD SOULS

People of Earth believe that there are old souls and young souls. However, all souls are old souls. Having existed forever inside a soul-substance that is taken from and added back to, in perpetuity. Many souls never reach the spirit realms and are returned to the soul substance where they will once again emerge at a given and predetermined time. They are allowed to swarm back into galaxies, star systems, and planets, where they begin again, their endless trials and errors in the physical realms of existence. Where lies the hope and anticipation of breaking the mold of ignorance and stubbornness, and earning wings of freedom in the higher spirit worlds.

SPACE-AGE EARTH

Earth has entered the space age, and it will be a place of extreme trials of endurance in hellish situations in hostile environments. Human souls will be tested in the darkness of space, more so than on good old solid ground on Earth. Having to exist in closed environments and inside space suits easily compromised by everything that moves in and around space. In space, everything travels at phenomenal speeds that are faster than bullets and deadlier.

Space will be a war zone for the humans who work and play in space during the next hundred-thousand earth years. Not much different than what it's been on Battleship Earth, the last few hundred thousand years.

In space humans will encounter strange bedfellows, which will tail humans and hide from them in the dark alleys of space, in a Jeckle and Hyde scenario. Mysterious hiding places abound in space for those with the technological means to unlock the hidden doors. Space creatures and beings are a mixture of real and mechanical, and knowing which is which will be a difficult task for humans. Probes sent out to monitor the humans from the too-numerous-to-know and comprehend, sources, have been watching and waiting for the human newcomers, who have only recently begun testing their legs out in the cosmic playgrounds.

A playground filled with big and very strange kids and their toys, who often don't appreciate the need to slow down and play nice with the little tikes from Earth. As is true with any playground there are good little boys and girls, and there are bullies. And the human tikes will have to learn the hard way how to get along with both groups. Even though humans will never really know or communicate openly with either group of extraterrestrial beings.

The good ETs can be protective but don't always interfere when bullies move in and harass beat up or even kill, those they don't want playing in "their" playground and defiling their territory.

All of space, and every rock, planet, and moon, is occupied and owned by some extraterrestrial organization or a consortium of Alien organizations. Humans will be allowed to integrate into limited arenas, but large sections of the star system will remain off limits to humans. Like the mythical Garden of Eden, humans will never be allowed to eat from the tree of knowledge, the tantalizing and most desirable foods hidden in the garden.

As has been true with conquering lands on Earth, over the centuries, is also true when conquering space. Humans will have to contend with other humans from Earth, who will also compete fiercely with each other for the treasures hiding in plain sight, out in space. Some human countries will band together and form consortiums of their own, and some will go it alone, for the monumental prize is huge.

Resources in space are limitless and will never deplete. Such limitless abundance is forever being churned out by the sun and ejected into space perpetually, through solar flares and other means unknown to humans. The sun has been in constant production mode for billions of years and has created a huge stockpile of base metals, and everything else in the periodic table that formed naturally or otherwise; and so much more. Every kind of material known and unknown, is freely available for the taking for those with the will and courage to go out and harvest the cosmic fields. Gas giant planets, also contribute to the production of massive amounts of materials dumped into the star system periodically. All planets and moons shed like cats and dogs, sluffing off materials into space via volcanism, and all the while collecting and accumulating tons of space dust and rocks, in the ongoing process of exchange.

Hostilities in space will not be over common resources but will be due to other circumstances, which are equally important to some cosmic beings existing in the neighborhood. Humans are biological machines with a product suitable and desirable to a segment of Alien beings, who have seeded and harvested multiple products from various races bred to serve peculiar purposes in the cosmos.

There are many levels of Alien beings, and numerous numbers of Alien beings, in this star system, vying for control of their perspective properties, planetary and biological properties. Of those multitudes of beings, there are some who are more invested in keeping a low profile than other Alien beings, who sometimes flaunt their existence without fear of retaliation. Nevertheless, all superior beings remain hidden (more or less) from view from other Aliens and humans alike, for logistical reasons.

Much of the Alien activities are conducted by probes and androids and other highly sophisticated gadgets, which operate independently as surveillance and to interact with other Alien gadgets, craft, beings and equipment, within the star system.

Some Alien beings remain hidden from view only from the newcomers (humans) by cosmic decrees and protocols. Some for their desires to keep out of sight and out of mind for the sole reason of maintaining the upper hand over other low life beings like themselves.

Compared with all the Alien species in the star system, humans are the most technologically challenged of the bunch. Humans have only recently stuck their periscopes into space for a peek of what's out there and have managed to see right past the activities of advanced beings taking place in the whole of the star system, the galaxy and the universe (can't see the forest for all the trees).

But most of what's out there has no interest in showing itself to humans and doesn't. Alien massive ships and their large kingdoms dominate every corner of space in this star system. It would be quite the alarming sight if Aliens ever did uncloak and showed themselves to humans.

Humans have yet to test the ice in the pond of space and are tip-toeing out into the unknown darkness with an abundance of excess fear and trepidation. Displaying paranoid extreme caution. Humans have little idea or understanding of what is out there and what challenges they will encounter. Down deep inside, humans know something large lurks in the big deep blackness of space; which feeds and legitimizes the paranoia and extreme caution.

Some world leaders in the know have an inkling of a few goings on in the darkness of space, concerning extraterrestrial fleets. But no idea of the extent and reasons for the dealings, activities and happenings on nearby planets and moons. What little knowledge any country has regarding types of Aliens lurking, watching and waiting, for humans to cross that threshold, that big dividing road that leads into space, and the realm where anything goes, is heavily guarded.

There will be human roadkill, both hostile and unintentional, directed at the newcomers to the space game. Space travel will toughen humans up to all the dangers they will face in the final frontier of the wildest west humans will ever know. The blatant and pervasive hostility of space travel and exploration will force humans to improve and innovate survival skills, techniques, and technology so that they can continue and prosper in the race to space.

Traditionally, wars require there be a recognizable enemy so that one can prepare a strategy to fight the enemy or enemies. Enemies, that has for centuries, pestered humans on their turf (Earth), without the average humans' knowledge, or humans being cognizant of such reality. Humans remain unaware that they had and continued to have adversaries as well as supporters, on Earth, and in the space around Earth.

161

Most humans will incorrectly assume they are battling the hazards of space travel and the unavoidable accidents that happen in the perils of space. Countries will also blame each other when things go afoul suspecting that some accidents are perpetrated by competing corporations and countries, due to the quest for the riches to be found out in space.

Space exploration will not be all war and gore, as is true on the planet Earth. There are wars flaring up all the time in some parts of the world, and most people are not aware or affected by the mayhem of those wars. It will be the same in space. Space is huge, and there is a lot of elbow room for a whole lot of beings and their machinery to move around unnoticed, without having to get into someone else's face (space).

Humans will not be in space in any significant numbers until the next century. And even then, humans will hardly have scratched the surface of space travel and exploration. Most human space activity will be near Earth, on the moon, and perhaps a little will be on Mars. Most space activities will be accomplished and performed by drones and robots that will construct hotels in orbit around the moon, Mars, and Earth. A few small colonies will spring up on the moon, by governments and private industries.

Humans mining for gold and other valuable metals and resources on moons and asteroids will be a negligible part of space exploration, compared to the real industrial bonanza that will expand space occupation in the latter part of this century, which is tourism. Tourism will draw humans into space in ever larger numbers as the cost of space travel drops precipitously, as more people get involved in space activities. The big economic payoff will be the supporting industries for tourism and space mining operations.

UTOPIA AND SEXUALITY

Utopia planets are nestled inside star systems with all the other planets circling the sun. But Utopia planets are not visible from the human-type planets and are made of a different substance than the visible rocky and gas planets. Rocky and gas planets are born from the star (sun). And will return to the sun when the sun expires and is recycled back into the cosmic matter of Black Holes, the givers and takers of star matter at the center of galaxies.

Utopias are not of the sun and will never cease existing when suns (stars) parish or diminish. Utopias migrate and visit new stars (suns) to play with and orbit around, and can travel on their own to other star systems at any time, guided by the spirit beings in charge of the utopias. Utopia planets control their orbits and can remain stationary for spectacular events put on by the sun or any other cosmic spectacle and phenomena, such as Black Holes, quasars, comets, Nebulae, etc.

Some utopia planets have the added features of procreation where human-type beings create families and enjoy all the pleasures available without the pain, fear, and frustrations that dampen the joy of family life on lower Earth type planets. Unlike Earth-type planets designed for learning, punishment and incarceration, utopia planets are designed for love and pleasure, only. On Earth, humans have to juggle jobs, money, crime, hate, wars, famine, diseases, envy, weather, death and a host of other things that make the enjoyment of life a challenge.

On utopia, families can spend precious quality time with each other, doing many types of activities together. Like taking vacations on marvelous and magical resorts all the time, not one week or two every year, if that. In utopia people never need to work for income because the worlds they live on are one hundred percent mechanized and robotic. Utopia planets outnumber all other types of planets in every star system in every galaxy in the universe. Utopia is the destination choice of most people who move up and out of reincarnation zones; before moving on to a pure spirit existence. Utopias are halfway houses for souls not yet prepared or willing to move out of the physical realms permanently.

Utopia existence is located on planets, moons, space cities, and on massive spaceships that are perpetually sailing the oceans of space. Utopias offer unlimited lifestyles and opportunities for every kind of reality available in the universe. Including reliving precious moments from past lives. Family members can join up and live the lives they enjoyed the most together while on Earth; waiting for each family member to join them after they move out of Earth existence.

One of the deepest pains on Earth is the feeling that such moments with loved ones will be gone forever after they die. Cherish-worthy-moments created during hectic lives on lower-level living, are preserved and can be reactivated any time during a utopia existence. Memories are stored and await the souls that have climbed out of the pits of death-planets to claim and relive with the very people they created the memories.

An equal amount of utopia planets have no procreation on them, and people exist their whole lives as young adults, never aging and never being sick. They do whatever pleasures them in work and life. People don't get married and enjoy gatherings and activities together or alone on splendid places with perfect living conditions of their choosing.

The universe pays for everything. The universe is immensely rich in everything imaginable. Has always been rich and will always be rich. The only reason poverty and sickness exist on some planets is that people tend not to value themselves and those around them. Such people remain consumed with envy and ignorance, instead of love and joy. Therefore are confined to Earth planets for the duration of their cherished delusions.

Nudity is common on all utopia planets, those with families and those without families. Everyone is nude, and clothing is "not" optional. The bodies people have on utopia planets are adapt to the conditions of the planets and have no need for restrictive covering or clothing for warmth, ego or show. Gorgeous sunny days and fairytale nights are the only weather on utopia. Perfect weather all the time because utopias are designed and built for perfect living.

Several versions of utopias exist. Some utopias are a few degrees above Earth life. And people on such utopias continue to work, learn and contribute to life on lower planets, helping develop technology and provide administrative services to the lower star systems and planets in each galaxy.

SEXUALITY

Sexuality is a creation by the Supreme Beings running the shows throughout the universe. Sexuality is the most natural and most innocent of all human and spirit interactions. Sexuality and nudity are the basis of life on all utopias, planets and places, where advanced beings, human and humanoid, enjoy the pleasures of each other's unhindered complexities.

Sexuality is a spiritual intrusion into the physical world; a gift of altruistic pleasure unconditionally given to humanity. Sexuality is engaged in and enjoyed by all levels of spirit beings while in the flesh or the multitudes of spirit realms. In the flesh sex serves two purposes, reproduction, and entertainment. In the spiritual world, it only serves as entertainment and endless enjoyment. Spirituality itself is a state of continuous ecstasy and becomes more so when like-minded souls interact lovingly and passionately with each other.

Negative spirits in the physical and the spirit world make many attempts to demonize and tarnish sexuality in the physical realms through religious doctrines and deceptions. Such practices propagate ignorance of human sexuality with false teachings that further perpetrate demagoguery against innocent people and their natural sexual desires.

168

Throughout most of human history, sex was viewed as a divine gift from the gods; it was the god of Abraham that commanded Abraham and his offspring to populate the world with their sex-induced seeds. For the sole purpose of fulfilling god's directive. Abraham collected many wives and concubines (slaves) as personal lovers, as did his sons Isaac and Jacob, per god's command and with god's blessing.

The three pillars of the three major religions, Judaism, Christianity, and Islam, all claim their roots from the patriarchs, Abraham, Isaac, and Jacob, and all three are the archetypes of sexual prowess and excesses concerning sexuality. God commanded these religious and righteous men to take on multiple wives and numerous female slaves, called concubines, in the holy books, and have sex with "all" of them to spread their seeds across the land. Godly acts that most men would have cherished doing with or without the promise from God of heavenly rewards for performing such righteous deeds.

In essence, lascivious sex is sanctioned from the highest realms of the universe. Which was the reality for sexuality before it was scandalized by the same religious leaders that sanctified it for themselves while demonizing it for their flocks of followers.

Sex was and still is about competition. Converting people to a religious belief is only one part of the equation for growing religious institutions. Making babies and raising them inside of a religious belief system is much faster and a far more productive way to grow religious institutions (cults).

Nevertheless, monogamy and responsibility are important virtues for modern societies to adhere to on Earth planets.

Because of religious distortions, sexuality had a falling out and became a thing of shame and perversion. The misunderstanding (intentional distortions) came in the misinterpretations of biblical accounts, stories, outright lies and religious dogma, about fictional places such as Sodom and Gomorra.

Sodom and Gomorra remain elusive to biblical historians, and historians in general, for the factual reasons that they were never real places on the map or the planet. Biblical historians only agree that Sodom and Gomorra were probably located on the southern edge of the Dead Sea, in the land of Canaan. And that's the clue to what Sodom and Gomorra were, a metaphor for the Jewish Promised Land, which is the ancient land of Canaan.

The land of Canaan was not a godless place where the inhabitants fornicated night and day with each other; it was the exact opposite. Canaan was a place where gods outnumbered people. Canaan was where people worshiped numerous gods and deities that were as varied and as numerous as the people who lived in Canaan. The numbers of deities that people worshiped were unimaginable and were exploited excessively by the people; to the point that the people became nonproductive and derelict in their daily duties and activities. Such realities were not exclusive to Canaan but were also true for the people and inhabitants in every country and village in the world; in antiquity as well as in modern times. Such worship of multiple gods and belief systems was normal back then, as it remains so to this day.

The driving force behind the droves of competing religious beliefs around the world is the millions of desperate people in search of some meaning in their lives. People wanted favors from the gods and prayed for better crops, and more cash-flow. The same desires that all people have struggled with throughout the ages. In other words, there was no disgraceful sex going on at Sodom and Gomorra or anywhere else, other than the normal sex that people engaged in daily; and did so in every city and town all over the world since people walked the face of the Earth.

Worshiping animals while people starved from lack of food is the real evil. Such religious perversions created

171

multitudes of wars that plagued the people of the world for centuries. Superstitions, delusions, falsehoods, and the need for scapegoats for crop failures, and other human maladies and tragedies rests fully on the shoulders of the perpetrators of religious dogma.

Temples were built to appease the angry gods with the sacrifice of people, animals, and property. In other words, it was a protection racket set up by religious leaders, who gained power and fear over the people, who were forced to pay dearly so that the gods didn't make their lives more miserable than they already were.

Sex was never the issue concerning Sodom and Gomora. The two fictional cities created by religious zealots, simply for the prize of gold and the control over multitudes of people around the globe. Sodom and Gomorra represent the lustful perversion of pagan gods (false gods) who have enslaved humans to their false and sugarcoated beliefs. All religions are pagan religions, false religions created by humans under the direction of Alien beings for specific purposes, wars mostly.

The gods created sex and mankind created lies about sex. People are needlessly tormented by sexual desires their whole lives, due to ancient and modern religious doctrine that had no rational meaning back in antiquity, and never has had any rational meaning in this modern, and so-called, enlightened period.

The Garden of Eden was the world before religious institutions became involved in the affairs of humans and turned natural sexual desires into evil desires that people needed to be saved from, for a price, to be paid at the collection plate or the pits of hell for all eternity. The sad part of this craziness is how easily so many people fall for such blatant silly lies.

Sex is a mechanism of nature, of ecology and with a never-ending cosmic purpose that is no accident of Darwinian natural selection but is orchestrated by and from the spirit world.

Humans, and most living, breathing, things are the result of orgasms; in essence, people are fundamentally orgasms in the flesh. Love is at the root of our being, the physical and spiritual part. Pure love is a byproduct of orgasm and is what binds those that share the experience forever. Love by itself does not create a strong bond as it does when mixed with sex. We love our friends, our parents, our siblings and our children, but the bond between lovers is the strongest bond.

The attachment with children, who come into our lives because of sex, and sometimes love, is also very strong. Sex is what humans do best, not by a fluke of nature but by purposeful design by higher beings, who created human bodies.

Humans did not create sex nor have they created the urges, desires, and the lust, which are the intrinsic elements of sex, by design, and the products of a higher order than mortal humans.

Of all the creatures on Earth, only humans have taken the burden upon themselves to feel guilt concerning the most natural and essential thing created in the universe, sex. Sex didn't use to be a twisted Jekyll and Hide conflagration of ecstasy and damnation.

SOULMATES

The idea of finding that special soulmate and enjoying each other in this life and for eternity has a basis in how this universe works. But is much more profound than finding that "one" person (soul). Soulmates number in the hundreds of thousands, if not a whole lot more, for some souls. Souls don't have only one soulmate they have a universe of soulmates to engage in and enjoy (if one wanted to). Friendships that are formed and allowed to develop and flourish on Earth planets is a means of expanding a soul family.

Such large numbers of intimate relationships are overwhelming and near impossible to grasp in the practical and the physical realms, as on Earth. Where making friends and keeping them can be a tremendous energy-sapping job, which easily cripples the endurance levels of the strongest and most tolerant of people. Souls remain unaware of the numbers of soulmates accumulated while alive and inside of physical bodies. Only becoming aware of the magnitude of soulmates they have after entering the spirit world, from where multitudes of mates are more manageable and in proper perspective.

Nonetheless, searching for that one soul mate while in the physical world is sensible. But searching is overstated, and choosing is what happens. People are surrounded by potential soulmates, souls from past lives and new soulmates that form during life experiences. Unfortunately, not all soulmates are fun to be around, or with, due to things that have transpired between souls in past lives or current lives. Whether or not such discrepancies are removed or smoothed over, depends on the two souls involved. Souls can choose to sever loose ends and remove incompatibles from the roster of soulmates.

One of the reasons for multiple lives, rebirths, and reincarnations, is to interact with other souls and become soulmates through trial and error. Souls make many friends and enemies during interactions with others. Some things must be mended between souls before they can be released from the binding physical world and enter the spirit world. Some souls manage to enter the spirit world with unfinished circumstances and find that they cannot advance to higher levels because of lingering regrets keeping them down. They are stuck and in denial about their predicament and roam the world as spectrums, ghosts, haunted and haunting places, where they have resided and created their obstacles, which deny them tranquility.

CELEBRITIES

Souls entering the physical realm don't mysteriously become popular celebrities out of the blue or from blood, sweat, and tears during their current lives. Millions of people work hard in hopes of becoming something or other, bigger than they are, and never do. Nor are they able to break the obstacles keeping them from fame and fortune, regardless of efforts spent (it still don't hurt to try). But wasting a lifetime trying to achieve something that stubbornly resist all efforts, is also unproductive. Cutting losses and trying something different never hurts and might brighten or create new horizons.

People who make it big in life had earned that privilege, status, and ability before they were born. The earned it in some previous life or lives. Their gravy train arrives at a predetermined time in their present life. It is a gift and sometimes a punishment. What separates one from the other is taking pleasure and thriving or squandering the gift and living a miserable life because of the gift. Such gifts or curses usually only last for the duration of one lifetime. After celebrities die their souls revert to normal, average, and typical spirit form, and enter the spirit stream moving up, down, or back to the flesh, as all souls do.

There are no celebrities in the whole of the universe. Only the illusion of celebrity that takes place on the low end, ego-entwined, Earth-type planets.

HUMANS

Humans don't own their bodies or emotions. After a certain time, those physical elements are stripped away, and the human dies; and then returns to where they came from, a spiritual world that exists in a higher dimension than the three-dimensional one most people have become addicted to. People call this fabled higher dimension paradise. Many don't believe that such places exist, and other people simply hope that there is "something" after this life, while remaining unsure.

Many people can't make that leap of faith due to the three-dimensional mindset they were born into. Making the leap in the here and now is not a prerequisite to spiritual growth because all people will make that leap in their own sweet time while alive. If not, then they certainly will at their moment of death.

Illusions and delusions have expiration dates too, and like a caterpillar throws off its cocoon and takes flight with new wings, so to the human soul will take flight from the human body, eventually.

Human bodies (soul containers) are the hardware; human emotions are the software that operates the hardware. The software is the preprogramming created by those who put people into their physical human bodies.

Human bodies that were created specifically for each person before they entered this plane of existence are the cocoons, where people procure spiritual wings, some faster than others.

What people see in the mirror is what they get, physically speaking. Some people make cosmetic modifications to circumvent nature's flaws through surgical procedures. Some people debase and abuse what they have been given, degrading their body and soul, and wasting a gift; a means to become better souls. People are free to do so as part of the free will contract. And like all contracts there are always loopholes and contingencies; the small print most people don't bother reading. Hunger pains, sexual desires, hate, love, and joy, are basic software that people receive at birth. How people use that software is what makes them who they are, and will determine where they go when they die.

Physical and emotional desires are software inside the human machine and not of our making. People crave, need, and want material things and pleasures because that is how they were built, to crave things. People can abuse the things that they ultimately blame on hormones, bad-hair-days, lust, food, and other stimulants. Bottom line, humans do not create desires, but humans can with a modicum of restraint, control desires.

Sexuality was created foremost for pleasure, not for procreation. Higher beings determine who will or will not participate in procreation (giving birth, having children); and the increase of the population of this planet is dictated from above, not the act of sex. Many sexually active people never have children. They were not "given" the gift or the burden of procreation.

The byproduct of sex is love between the partners, and often the creation of offspring, which are gifts from the spirit world. Giving birth is a privilege that allows people to bring into their lives loved ones from past lives or to add new souls to their eternal clan.

The pure love we see in a baby's eyes at birth is simply a family reunion, loved ones coming together again from other dimensions and time zones. Not all family reunions end up happy reunions. That too is not by accident. Many of the people we come to know in our lives are people we have known in previous lives. Some of these acquaintances are good some are not. Injustices done to others in past lives can follow us to this life. The opposite is also true.

"Do on to others as they have done on to you" is not a good policy, if revenge is what is happening, which can lead to a vicious cycle of reincarnation to undue. Always do better by others regardless of what evil they do to you—if you wish to break the chain of hatred and revenge. Revenge is a plague that follows people from one life to the next, for eternity, in some case.

Life on Earth is not utopia, and it never was meant to be utopia. Earth is not a designated utopia planet. People are sent to Earth to struggle and suffer and to know and experience mental and physical pain; that they have caused to others during past lives. People are here because of difficulties from past mistakes and have been given opportunities to rectify whatever blunders brought them to Earth in the first place. It would be easy if people knew what those discrepancies in past lives were so that they could rectify them and get off this rock, but that is not allowed, and most people remain clueless of what they are here to fix, and why.

The reason is that life is a blind test. A sting operation carried out by beings more evolved than humans are. Knowledge of such virtue-traps is privileged information that only falls into the hands of a select few— those that can grasp and take advantage of such gifts are the few.

It's not so much as what took place in a past life that keeps people from progressing to higher plains of existence. It's what they do in their present circumstances in the here-and-now that determines their trajectory.

Souls that can't move up because of barriers put in place by higher echelon spirits are doomed to hang out on Earth planets, and create mischief and mayhem wherever they travel. Evil spirits swarm around lower planets and torment humans who possess good souls and are prime candidates to leave Earth, at the end of their existing life if they don't stumble.

Evil spirits are discouraging beings, always attempting to trip people up and cause them to falter over the smallest of infractions. Road-rage is a good example and has caused otherwise good people to lose control for only a moment, enough to ruin their lives and the lives of others.

Demon spirits are empowered by the evil that radiates from the millions of evil people imprisoned on Earth. They are the souls that have allowed themselves to be manipulated by evil and deceptive leaders, whose jobs are to entice naive people to hate, despise and envy good people.

FLEET OF CARRIAGES

I have a huge fleet of carriages (UFOs) at my beckoning. At my command carriages sail across the galaxy and into star systems and onto planets and pluck souls from their slumber and bring them to me. My carriages made of godly materials are unknown to anyone but the makers, creators of the magical crafts, brought to existence by me. All Super beings and their lieutenants have their fleets of carriages created by themselves to perform specific duties in the cosmos. All carriages are unique creations and made of similar materials and designs. Carriages are impenetrable and cannot be entered or exited by any beings and creatures human or otherwise, only I and others like me can place and remove beings, people, and souls from carriages. Propulsion systems of carriages energize by the spirits who created the carriages.

Super beings have immense energy reserves within themselves, far more than stars, and never deplete. Carriages use no fuels or materials from the world of three-dimensional matter and operate solely on the energy of Superbeings. Carriages could be chambers of horror or places of heavenly delights (manifestations created by Super beings), depending on the souls that are summoned and placed into the carriages. I interfaced with thousands of human souls at any gathering and have multiple gatherings to attend to besides humans, nonstop. As do endless numbers of other spirits in my caste of Superbeings.

Human souls seized during sleep, and the physical souls seized throughout the day and night get transported to me at a moment's notice inside of my carriages. From where they traveled safely and unimpeded, instantly across the cosmos to any location inside the galaxy at my sole discretion and choosing.

I showed my clients (abductees) what they looked like from the spirit's perspective, opening up their souls as performing an autopsy on them while alive, and them looking on; which is gut-wrenching and horrendous for all souls to see and experience. After such an experience, and if I'm feeling generous, I sometimes treat the souls to a wonderland of sights inside of their perspective star systems. And let them see and enjoy a taste of some of the wonders of the universe. Wonders that are waiting for them when they too escape from their chains of ignorance, pettiness and irrelevant beliefs that hold so many people back. So many people trapped by delusions that steal the pleasurable realities of existence from them. Even as people learn these new traits while inside my ships, they will mostly never show them to the world at large. Permitting ideal concepts they have learned to soak in and grow within their souls that ultimately helps them to mature during their entrapment in the physical realms, the corona of hell (Earth).

A sampling of the visitors to my carriages

MARY

Mary Sue, was a good church going woman, had three children, all well behaved, and a husband that earned a good living. She was a housewife and did volunteer work at her church. She was taken one night during her sleep and placed into my carriage. Her body remained in her bed with her husband, who was made to remain asleep. While she was absent from her body, her body became restless.

Mary believed she was in a dream and taken to places of her past in other lives and also shown places that she would go to after her present life ended. Places she would go to were contingent on a few details she had yet to confront. She kept putting it off, hoping it would resolve itself and go away.

Early in her marriage she cheated on her husband, and it was eating her up alive. She never did it again. It was a moment of weakness when her husband was out of town on business. A member of the church offered to keep her company one night, and they drank a little wine. The children were very young and unaware of her lustful adventure.

Mary knows too well one of her husband's weaknesses, that he is a very jealous man, and would never forgive her if he found out; even if she confessed and told him how sorry she was. The deed itself was not a stain on Mary's soul, the years of anguish and guilt eating away at her, was. Her sincere remorse absolved her deed. But Mary couldn't move forward while her predicament festered inside of her.

I brought Mary's mother into the picture. She had passed away a few years earlier and was a good soul and living her life in utopia. She was the soul that requested this intervention. Mary's mother explained her options to remove this dark cloud over Mary's head all these years. "Forgive yourself and forget," she told her daughter, Mary. Upon hearing those words from her long dead mother, exploded in tears (soul tears) and relief flooded into her soul. The job was done! And Mary's soul was returned to her body.

Typical Alien abductions are anything but typical. However, they do share similarities on several levels. Most of the people abducted have no idea that such things happen. And especially not to them, if they did believe in such things. Most people associate abductions to bad dreams or very pleasant dreams but dreams nonetheless.

Some people view abductions as demons who have come to torment or take possession of people's bodies and souls. However, the vast majority of humanity has no idea about the UFO phenomena or Alien abductions. Most people don't believe it happens, and could care less about such unknowable things.

Ignorance is not bliss, but it can be, and that is why most people intentionally are kept ignorant about the doings (intrusions), and the comings and goings, of the spirits in the physical worlds.

People with an inkling of the paranormal and the Alien invasion taking place on Earth, are more open to the possibilities of having direct encounters with Alien beings. Some people look forward to such dealings and encounters, and others are horrified at the thought of such dreadful prospects.

Those dreading contact have heard horror stories about the demon-beings and didn't know anything about them and don't want to know anything about them.

Demon beings are real and often found inside of my carriages. Once a person is fetched (abducted) it is for a reason. And searching for demons is one of the popular reasons.

Demons are tricky and can hide right in front of people without the person having any clue they are stalked (A very unpleasant feeling for most humans). More so when the demon creatures are inside of a freaky UFO (carriage).

A carriage is a place of wonder and adventure. It's crazy mind boggling just how much weird stuff can squeeze inside of a small carriage. Carriages have no real size to them, other than illusions that are projected by carriages themselves. Often people report what they see as saucer shaped and sometimes carriages have bulges at the top or bottom or both. And the typical size of flying saucers is about thirty feet wide, more or less.

All that stuff is illusions projected by the Alien UFO craft, carriage. Carriages are masters of illusions.

Not a single carriage is like another carriage. A unique spirit crafts each commissioned carriage. And spirits come and go and often take their unique plans with them when they go away and do something else altogether. In this grand universe of multiple opportunities and delights. Super spirits do that all the time (leave).

Allowing new spirits to get a feel of the massive ongoing soul projects throughout the galaxy, and get their hands dirty in the morass of human-type existence, from a higher perspective.

My personal fleet of carriages are not cookie-cutter, and neither are carriages of other spirits doing these tedious jobs. Each and every UFO is unique and a work of magical art and craftsmanship. Some carriages are used only once, having been fashioned specifically for a special client soul. Those are not a few and rare occasions and happen quite often. Nevertheless, each carriage conforms itself to fit each soul that it plucks out of bed, or wherever, and brings them to me for a sit-down chat.

I sometimes get carried away, where was I? Oh, yes, in search of pesky demons that have terrorized planet Earth for centuries, and so many millennia too. Millions of years this evil plague has tormented endless humans for pleasure and profit. Why the gods allow such things is privileged information that is seldom put out into the public arena.

Whenever one of my carriages captures a demon I'm alerted immediately. I then show up in person and put on attire I feel appropriate for the situation at hand. I take on human form, or any number of Alien forms and identities, such as Greys, tall whites, short blues, reptilian, the tooth fairy, Santa Clause or whatever the newest fad in the human belief system might be, I can become. By far the most popular disguises are religious icons and secular icons too. Any form or caricature I need be, I am.

DEMON

The ship, my carriage, isolates the demon inside one of the many rooms the ship has within it until I arrive. As soon as I'm able to be there, I begin questioning the demon. What's its name, how many names does it use? Why is it pestering so and so? And so on. The demon rarely cooperates and screams, kicks and curses at me. Eventually, I wear the demon down, and it begins to show fear. Fear that turns into terror, and it swiftly spirals down from there. The demon reaches a point that it weeps uncontrollably and finally begs for help and some direction in its perverted life. It desperately wants redemption, forgiveness for the atrocities it has committed against humans and humanity too.

I'm not in the forgiving business; that's some other dude's department. I summon my assistant who is in charge of this particular carriage and turn the matter over to it or them. It or them are often confused by patrons as being Grey Aliens, or any number of Alien creatures, by people who have reported Alien abductions. And that's fine, as long as it and them do their jobs. Which they do very well and often outdoing themselves with a slam-bang of a performance worthy of Oscars.

I hardly ever stick around for the final performance, although, sometimes I do. I always am confident that I'm leaving the demon in good and caring hands. Otherwise I would stay. But I receive summons constantly and so I'm off to deal with endless other situations in the cosmic battlefield.

The Grey (and company [it or them]) makes arrangements with the demon that the Grey deems appropriate to achieve resolution or a starting point towards some resolution. The demon reluctantly agrees to the terms and is returned to his bed (where he or she was snatched from earlier), in his house and to his family, with enough time to get some restful sleep and be up and on time to go to his regular job. This particular demon happened to be a lawyer. But similar demons can be found in most any occupation (if they have an occupation, many don't). It's not the occupation per se that people choose that makes them evil; it's what's inside the person's soul that makes them what they are. Extracting raw sewage from the soul is the reason most people are on lowlife planets such as Earth.

Sometimes I perform such drastic procedures in my carriage, but it's an unholy mess that requires a lot of cleanups afterward. Anyway.

TOM

A man in his fifties (Tom) is in a waiting room and expecting to see a newborn baby that a friend of his was delivering that day. The man is in my carriage and unaware of his circumstances. He is in his physical body and not in a dream. He was picked up by one of my trusty assistants from his bedroom while he was asleep and is in his night attire. Tom is fully awake, but my carriages are supernatural machines and chock full of more magic than Aladdin's lamp, and he only sees what I want him to see. I create whatever scenes I need to facilitate the message I hope to get across or that I wish to bring to life for Tom, during the interview.

Tom has met his requirements to move on with his life on another level. He is coming back to Earth as a superstar musician (his life's desire). His new body was delivered by his new mom a day earlier, and he was allowed to see the baby before being placed into it tomorrow. Tom was delighted to hold this new baby, the new arrival to this world, and had many questions for me on his mind. I told him that he would be that baby very soon. Tom was puzzled by my comment to him. I didn't need to clarify it any further. I told Tom that he would be returned to his bed and that he would die of a heart attack that morning. Tom returned to his bed with the help of my assistant. And be joined with his new family that evening. Tom didn't know what I was saying to him. And it didn't matter. Life goes on without most people's knowledge or awareness.

JAN

I meet on some level of awareness with most souls captured by my carriage. This next soul was picked up by one of my many soulless associates beforehand and she was prepped for my arrival. Jan was a bitter woman whose life was one misfortune after another. Jan could never catch a break, she told me. She believed she was in a dream, a nightmare, where she had a strange encounter with a man who was chasing her and was going to steal her purse, she believed. And she got into her car and drove very fast and lost control of her car, which then went over a cliff, and the car exploded, and Jan died.

Jan said she usually wakes up from that kind of dream and didn't know why she was still in the dream. She wanted badly to wake up, she told me.

I asked Jan about her life and what she thought about it, and the people she rubbed elbows with during her daily affairs. "She didn't trust anyone and most people didn't like her," Jan told me. Jan couldn't understand why. Jan didn't like most of the people she met through the years either. "They were all bigots and chauvinists, and she just hated them all," Jan yelled.

I showed Jan a short clip of a previous life she had. Jan was a man, a brutal man who also had a difficult life. He was a hardworking man working on a ship. Most of his time he spent on the ship, and every two weeks, if he was lucky, the boat captain gave him and his crewmates a leave. Shore leave so that he and the crew could spend some time at home with families. He didn't have any children but was married to a local girl he met in town a few years earlier. He didn't spend much time with his wife because of his work. She was a good wife and dedicated to him. But he loved drinking with his shipmates, and they always got drunk and into fights at the pub. By the time he got home, it was always late, and he was always in a no good of a mood to be ragged on by his wife. Mostly when his wife whined that she fixed him a dinner, now cold. And he did what he often did; he beat his wife for no reason at all. He hated that about himself, but he easily lost his temper and his control when drunk.

Not knowing that the clip shown to Jan was her in her past life, she said, "I know men who are like that too!" They are animals and should be locked up in cages where they belong. I told Jan that the man was her in a life before the one she had now. What I said didn't register in her mind. And she asked why there were animals in her house. "There was a wild boar, a tamed pig, a donkey and a goat," Jan told me. Jan never asked who I was, and I didn't tell her. I was only a voice in her dream. Jan and the animals were inside of my carriage. Something Jan couldn't know or understand and believed she was still dreaming.

Jan screamed, "I want to wake up!" I told her she had died in a car accident and was going to be returned to Earth in a few years, and would be a girl and live a better life than the one she just lost in the car crash. I let Jan pick which animal she preferred to live inside of until her next life as a human in a few years. Jan got agitated, and I told her to remain calm. Jan calmed down and pointed at the goat.

Hey you, the reader, what's in your soul? Pencil me in; I'll see you soon...

BOOKS BY THE AUTHOR

In League with a UFO......................1997

Shrouded Chronicles....................….....2000

A Day with an Extraterrestrial..........2006

An Italian Family, Capisce?.............2011

Israel Crucified................................2012

Orphans of Aquarius........................2012

UFOs in the Year of the Dragon.......2012

Mars and the lost planet Man.........2014

Graduation into the Cosmos..........2016

BLOGS IN BOOK FORM

UFOs and Extraterrestrials are as real as the nose on your face...2005...Published in book form in 2011

Coming clean on Extraterrestrials and the UFO Hidden Agenda...2007-8

Part 1...2011

Part 2...2012

Part 3...2012

Part 4...2012

Part 5...2013

Part 6...2013

Websites:

ufolou.com

baldin.proboards.com

FACEBOOK. Lou Baldin